FALLING STAR ENCHANTMENT

The Cambion Club, Book 3

Anne Rollins

ARE YOU SIGNED UP FOR DRAGONBLADE'S BLOG?

You'll get the latest news and information on exclusive giveaways, exclusive excerpts, coming releases, sales, free books, cover reveals and more.

Check out our complete list of authors, too!

No spam, no junk. That's a promise!

Sign Up Here

www.dragonbladepublishing.com

Dearest Reader;

Thank you for your support of a small press. At Dragonblade Publishing, we strive to bring you the highest quality Historical Romance from some of the best authors in the business. Without your support, there is no 'us', so we sincerely hope you adore these stories and find some new favorite authors along the way.

Happy Reading!

CEO, Dragonblade Publishing

Additional Dragonblade books by Author Anne Rollins

The Cambion Club
Garden Folly Magic (Book 1)
Twelfth Night Sorcery (Book 2)
Falling Star Enchantment (Book 3)

Beau Monde Secrets Series
Secrets at Selwyn Castle (Book 1)
Discovery at Dogwood Cottage (Book 2)
The Incident at Ingleton (Book 3)
The Case at Castle Rock Cove (Book 4)

CHAPTER ONE

February, 1817

"**D**ORA," LADY GRANTLY said, "you are probably wondering why I called you here."

Lady Grantly sat upright, not even letting her back touch the cushions, even though she had taken the most comfortable chair in her private sitting room. She ignored the leather ottoman in front of the wingchair, preferring to rest her feet primly on the floor.

Lady Grantly looked every inch the respectable widow, from the neat mobcap on the top of her silvered hair to her pretty black slippers. Though she had been out of mourning for a year, she wore a lavender gown suitable for half mourning.

She'd probably realized that the color did wonders for her complexion, Dora thought cynically.

"I did wonder," Dora admitted. "Am I in trouble again? What did I do?" She could not remember doing anything deserving of a lecture. But she also knew that her definition of *deserving of a lecture* differed from Lady Grantly's definition.

For example, Dora was all too aware that at this very moment, there were mud stains on the back of her new pelisse. She had unwisely sat on the ground to watch her youngest siblings try to fly a kite. They succeeded, but only because Dora had cast an impromptu spell on the kite, making it fly despite the lack of wind. She regretted neither the time she spent with Clarinda and Jack nor her surreptitious use of magic, but she did regret that she hadn't thought to bring a cushion or blanket outside to protect her clothing.

Most likely, her new pelisse would be permanently stained. Worse, it was the second garment she'd ruined this week. Two days ago, she'd scorched one of her walking gowns by standing too close to the fire after an invigorating but rainy tramp about the wilderness. If Lady Grantly found out, she might very well decide that Dora needed to be restricted to the house again.

Dora did not like restrictions.

"Not at all. But please take a seat. We have much to discuss." Lady Grantly's blue eyes looked placid and calm. Even so, Dora steeled herself for something unpleasant.

Lady Grantly gestured at the least comfortable chair in the room: a wooden armchair with a worn leather seat. Sir Isaac Grantly had been inexplicably fond of it, which was the only reason it had never been discarded. After his death, his widow had preserved the chair in his memory, though it looked out of place next to Lady Grantly's newer, lushly upholstered armchair and sofa. Dora and her siblings called the chair "the Throne of Disgrace," because it was inevitably where a penitent child was forced to sit after any wrongdoing.

So, Dora *was* in trouble. Since there was no point in delaying the inevitable, she obediently sat down. She crossed her feet at the ankles and rested her folded hands on her lap, doing her best to project an image of ladylike propriety. She was quite good at this, having had years of practice, but it was nevertheless an act. Nearly everything she did in Lady Grantly's presence was an act.

"What do you wish to discuss, ma'am?" she asked. Honora, Belinda, Clarinda, and Jack all called Lady Grantly *Mama*, but Dora did not. As far back as she could remember, she had known that Lady Grantly was not *Mama* to her, though Sir Isaac had never minded her calling him *Papa*.

Lady Grantly's smile remained cool and detached. "It is about your future, my dear. It is time we made some changes."

Dora's heart began to pound more heavily, but she refused to let the polite smile fall off her face. "Indeed?" Was she about to be sent off to live with Aunt Sarah? There had been some talk of that last fall, but nothing had come of the plan. *Please, not that!* Dora silently begged. Aunt Sarah was kind, but she was very religious, and she expected her guests to join her for lengthy prayers every day.

"Yes, indeed." Lady Grantly nodded. "You will be nineteen in a few months, Dora. You are no longer a child. I think it is time we made some provision for the rest of your life. Your fortune will not be adequate to sustain you, as you must know."

Dora swallowed. She *really* wasn't going to like this conversation, was she? "I suppose you are right," she replied.

Though, in truth, she did not consider her financial situation desperate. Her father had bequeathed her three thousand pounds in the funds, just as he had done for his legitimate daughters. Many gentlewomen possessed less.

"Therefore, I have been looking for employment for you. I am pleased to report that I have found an ideal position at Hetherage Hall."

"A position?" Dora kept her voice level, refusing to let her doubt, confusion, or anger slip out. What on earth was Lady Grantly going on about now?

No one had ever suggested that Dora would need to seek employment. At Miss Merton's Academy, most of the girls who planned to teach stayed on at the school as under teachers for a year or two. Dora had not done so. No one had ever so much as hinted that she ought to. She might have taken her marks a little more seriously if she'd thought she would one day need a teaching reference.

"Yes." Lady Grantly nodded briskly. "I don't know what you know about Hetherage Hall, but it has an extensive magical garden. A magician is needed to manage the stillroom. I thought you would be ideal for that position."

"You thought I would be ideal for a position as a stillroom maid?" Dora's perfect-young-lady façade cracked, spilling dismay into her voice

Papa would never have allowed this! Sir Isaac's will had made it very clear that Dora was to be educated as a gentlewoman, despite her ignoble birth. Sir Isaac had probably hoped that his second daughter would marry into a comfortable establishment, but he had made provisions in case that did not happen. In addition to her own fortune, Dora was guaranteed an allowance from the estate so long as she remained unmarried. There was no need for her to go into service.

"It is a position for a *magician*," Lady Grantly reminded her, as if that made the suggestion more palatable. "You would not be asked to scrub dishes or empty chamber pots. You would mix teas and brew potions. It is more like being a domestic alchemist, I suppose." She smiled, pleased by her own argument.

Dora was less pleased. "But that isn't even the kind of magic I work!" she protested. "I am a *sorceress*, not a witch. Besides, I have no talent for medicinal magic." Manipulating physical objects through magic? Yes. Brewing medicines? No. Sorcery, unlike wizardry or witchcraft, did not require the use of herbs or crystal.

Lady Grantly dismissed these concerns with a wave of her hand. "I have already spoken to the Duke of Belmont. He agrees that you would be ideal for the position."

For one frightening moment, Dora forgot to breathe. She was a little surprised that her heart kept pounding. "The Duke of Belmont?" She whispered, hoping she had misheard.

"Oh, yes. He owns Hetherage Hall. Didn't you know?"

Dora mutely shook her head. She knew Belmont owned properties all across England, but Belmont Court was the only estate she could name. She had never seen Belmont Court in person; she had not been invited to the Twelfth Night masquerade at which her older sister disappeared. She was a little surprised that someone as important as the Duke of Belmont even remembered she existed. They had met at a few social events, but he never deigned to notice Dora. He had eyes only for Honora.

"You will leave in two days' time," Lady Grantly continued.

"That should give you time to prepare. You will not need ball gowns or evening gowns, merely some simple clothing for everyday wear. Have you any questions?"

"Um." Dora hemmed and hawed, trying to buy enough time to think of a good argument. "What if I prefer a different sort of work?"

If she must earn her keep, she would rather be a magic teacher at a girl's school. Sir Isaac had taught her both practical and theoretical sorcery, and she knew much more about magical theory than most magic mistresses. That was not arrogance, but simple fact.

"You never know. You might find that you enjoying managing a still room," Lady Grantly suggested. "In any case, your uncle and I insist that you give this position a try."

"My uncle agrees with you?" Dora's heart sank. Uncle Robert was her legal guardian. If he supported this plan, there would be no one to whom she could appeal.

Lady Grantly nodded. "Mr. Grantly knows how important it is for our family to remain in the Duke of Belmont's good graces."

"Why is that important?" Dora demanded. Yes, the duke was both wealthy and powerful, but what did he have to do with the Grantly family? Their paths had rarely intersected until he met Honora at a hunt ball last fall.

"That is none of your concern. Remember, Dora, a proper young lady does not show unseemly curiosity about things that do not concern her." A line formed between Lady Grantly's eyebrows. "Your older sister has been a bad influence on you. I hope you are not going to start asking impertinent questions the way she does."

"No, ma'am. I know better than to do that." Dora continued to speak deferentially, though she would rather have blown a raspberry at Lady Grantly.

Honora was no more inquisitive than Dora; she just lacked the social sense necessary to tell when she could or could not get away with her questions. In any case, Dora's question had to do with a matter that most certainly *did* concern her. If she was to be sent to work at one of Belmont's estates, shouldn't she know why?

"Have you any more questions?" Lady Grantly still frowned at her, although even her frown looked elegant. Lady Grantly's ability to look dainty, ladylike, and genteel even when behaving nastily was one of the things Dora chiefly hated about her.

"No, ma'am." Dora had many questions, but she did not think Lady Grantly was likely to answer them honestly. What she really needed to do was come up with a *plan*. She could best do that on her own.

Or with the assistance of the right friend. Already, the germ of an idea teased at the back of her mind.

GRANTLY COTTAGE SAT at the edge of the park, within the palings but in sight of the road. Tom Robson, the steward's son, liked to joke that his eagle-eyed grandmother kept better watch over the estate than a Royal Guardsman would have. He might have been right, at that.

Dora was such a frequent visitor that the maid who answered the door did not bother to ask what brought her there. "Master Tom is working on account books in the study," she told Dora. "You know the way, miss?"

They both knew perfectly well that Dora could find her way to the study. Dora knew the way to every room in the cottage, including the third-story room where she and Tom had once nearly started a fire when they knocked over the footlights for their homemade stage.

But when she reached the study, Tom was not precisely welcoming. "Go away," he grumbled. "I'm working. Some of us have work to do, you know."

Dora ignored his non-greeting and sank down into the scruffy leather armchair near the fire. It was far more comfortable than the Throne of Disgrace.

"I will have work to do, too, if I don't find a way to avoid it." She lounged back in the chair, stretching her feet out to warm them by the fire.

"Oh, is your stepmother going to make you darn your own stockings now?" Tom did not bother to look up from his account book. Math had never been his favorite subject, and he struggled with keeping accounts. Rather unfortunate, given how important the skill was to a land steward.

"Worse than that! My evil stepmother is sending me off to be a still room maid at Hetherage Hall. She wants me to work for the Duke of Belmont," Dora explained.

Tom snorted, shook his head, and continued to scan the accounts.

"I'm not joking," Dora insisted. "I really am going to be sent away to become a servant."

Tom finally lifted his eyes from the pages of numbers he'd been double-checking. He took one look at Dora, and his expression changed. He took off his spectacles, rubbed his eyes, and put them back on, as if that might make the situation more reasonable.

"I don't think Lady Grantly can do that," he said at last. "Not legally. Didn't your father's will specify that you were to be raised the same as his other daughters?"

"It didn't say that I was his daughter at all," Dora reminded him. "It only referred to me as his ward." Even in death, Sir Isaac had refused to acknowledge his paternity.

This was such an old complaint that Tom did not bother responding. He merely waited for her to answer the real question.

"But yes," Dora conceded. "I am supposed to be educated, clothed, and provided for just like my sisters. I don't think the will specifically prohibits me being employed as a maid, though."

Sir Isaac would never have thought that possible. Dora doubted he had ever guessed how much his wife had despised his love child. Or if he guessed, he never addressed it—which made him complicit in Lady Grantly's treatment of Dora, didn't it? She preferred to think he did not know. After all, Lady Grantly was a good actress in her own way.

"What are you going to do, then?" Tom asked. "Consult a lawyer? You'd probably have to find a new one. You couldn't expect your father's solicitor to represent you."

It was Dora's turn to snort. That was exactly the sort of solution Tom *would* think of. "I might do that eventually, but first I am going to run away from home."

Tom gaped at her for a long moment. Then he closed his mouth and shook his head. "That is a *terrible* idea."

"It worked for Honora!" she reminded him.

Rather than become betrothed to the Duke of Belmont, the eldest Grantly daughter had run away with a wealthy nobleman no one else in the family had even met. Honora married Lord Valance the next day, thus freeing herself from her mother's manipulation. Dora had been rather jealous. Not of the marrying-a-stranger part—that seemed like rather a large gamble, though of course it might also have been exciting—but of the escaping-Lady-Grantly part. One might say she found her older sister's actions inspiring.

"Not every runaway fares as well as she did," Tom pointed out.

Dora could not argue with that. "I don't expect to elope with a viscount." She was not at all sure that she would like that, anyway. "But I could at least run off to London to make sure everything is well with Honora."

Dora had had no contact with Honora since the letter arrived revealing her marriage; Lady Grantly had forbidden all such correspondence. Dora could not help worrying about her sister. What if Lord Valance was no better than Belmont?

"I suppose that might work," Tom said doubtfully. "But Lady

Grantly will almost certainly send someone after you."

"Probably," Dora admitted. Lady Grantly never liked being defied, especially not by Dora. "That's why I should travel in disguise, don't you think?"

"Disguised as what?" Tom looked baffled.

She grinned at her friend, who ought to have known her well enough to guess. "As Theodore Rossini, of course."

"Oh, God no!" Tom buried his face in his hands. "Dora, that would never work!"

"Yes, it would," she argued. "I've done it before."

When a young lady who disliked restrictions lived in a world full of confining rules and expectations, she had to be creative in order to get what she wanted. Dora had learned to be very creative.

"You've gone about in disguise for a few *hours*. Not for days." Tom crossed his arms over his chest and gave her what he probably imagined was a stern look. In fact, he just looked constipated.

"It doesn't take days to get to London, Tom," Dora pointed out. They lived in Kent, not the Outer Hebrides. "And I disguised myself as a boy for an entire day last summer, remember?"

Just the thought of that day put a smile back on her face. She and Tom had hitched a ride in the back of a farm wagon, visited a local fair, and watched a horse race. It had been grand. Certainly, it had been worth being grounded at home for a week afterward. Of course, Lady Grantly had not known the whole story. If she had realized where Dora had gone or how she had been dressed, the punishment would have been harsher.

"Yes, but I was with you the whole time," Tom protested. "If you had gotten into any trouble, I could have helped you. That's different from traveling to London alone! How would you even get there?"

"On the stage. How else?" Really, that was a foolish question. So far as she could see, Tom's objections were all nonsense. What trouble did he imagine that she would get into that could be resolved with his help? He could not even work magic! Dora, on the other hand, had learned a few basic defensive spells from her father. She was perfectly capable of protecting herself.

"But you can come to London with me, if you like." She'd assumed she'd have to travel on her own, but shared adventures were often more fun.

"You know I can't do that." Tom stared down at the account book, looking almost regretful. "I am supposed to leave for Graystone Farm in a few days, remember?"

Dora's face fell. "Oh, I forgot about that."

Last year, Tom had begged his parents to let him study estate management instead of attending Oxford or Cambridge as they had wanted. His father had agreed only on condition that Tom actually learn what he needed to know for his chosen line of work. An experienced steward himself, Mr. Robson designed a grueling series of assignments for his son that included not just account books, but a stint of clerking for a local solicitor. Now, Tom was to take a turn laboring on a farm.

Frankly, Dora thought Tom would have had an easier time at Oxford, but he disagreed.

"Besides, it really wouldn't be good for your reputation to be discovered traveling alone with me." Tom averted his eyes. "People would assume—you know." A faint touch of pink illuminated his cheekbones.

"That is ridiculous! You don't fancy me, do you?" She knew for a fact that Tom preferred fair hair over dark hair. He particularly favored plump, pink-cheeked blonde girls—like her sister Belinda. His infatuation had to remain a secret, though. Neither Lady Grantly nor Uncle Robert would have thought a steward's son was an acceptable suitor.

"Well, no, but—"

"I suppose it would be difficult to convince other people of that," she admitted. The people who would be appalled at Dora wearing breeches would also be certain that a marriageable young lady could not simply be friends with a young bachelor.

The rules of propriety did not make exceptions for friends who had known each other all their lives.

Tom rumpled his hair and glared at her. "It would be *impossible* to explain! And that is beside the point. I can't run away with you. I have too much to do!"

Dora sighed. Tom was a dear boy, but she sometimes found him lacking in spirit. "I suppose not. In that case, I will just have to go by myself. All I need is for you to lend me some clothes."

Tom had grown taller and heavier than her, but the clothes he'd worn just a couple of years ago fit her perfectly. His old garments were supposed to be kept in storage for when his younger brother grew into them, but they had a habit of disappearing from the cedar chest when Dora and Tom were in need of adventure.

He narrowed his eyes. She narrowed hers back. They silently stared at each other for a long, tense moment.

Tom dropped his gaze, silently yielding. "I ought to send you packing back to Grantly Manor," he grumbled.

"No, you oughtn't," Dora retorted. "You know perfectly well that what Lady Grantly intends is wrong. You don't want me to be sent off to serve the Duke of Belmont, do you?"

"Of course not." His shoulders slumped. "Oh, all right. I'll see what I can find. Do you only need the one outfit, or should I pack a change of clothes?"

Dora grinned. "Just one, I should think. I imagine I will wear dresses again when I get to London. But can I borrow that blue-green waistcoat of yours? It matches my eyes." It was really too fine a garment to be worn for travel, but she had coveted it from the moment she saw it.

Tom rolled his eyes. "As if that mattered! A waistcoat is a waistcoat!"

Now it was Dora's turn to sigh. Would Tom never learn to appreciate good tailoring? "The right colors can make all the difference," she reminded him. "For example, that yellow dress I wore last spring made me look like a patient on her deathbed. But that shade of blue—"

Tom waved her into silence. "You can have whatever you want if you stop lecturing me," he promised.

Dora held her tongue, knowing she had gained her point. The path before her beckoned; she could not wait to get on her way. She would catch the first stage to London tomorrow morning. She would find her older sister and make sure that everything in the Valance household was really aboveboard. And she planned to enjoy herself thoroughly while doing all of it.

It was a pity Tom could not accompany her, though. She would've liked having a companion. But perhaps she would meet interesting people on the way. One never knew what might happen during an adventure.

CHAPTER TWO

Three Days Later

"**B**UT IF YOU need a sorcerer to help with the meteorite spell," Hannah Carrington said, "why didn't you just ask Oliver?" She sat on the sofa in the morning room at Carrington Abbey, her feet curled up beside her. Though she held an open book, she had not looked at it in at least ten minutes.

Her older brother sighed and leaned back in his chair, though *he* kept his feet on the floor rather than lounging like a housecat. "Valance and I do not work well together," he admitted. "Not when it comes to casting spells."

Peregrine and his former housemate could study together, play chess together, and *discuss* magic, but attempting even simple collaborations somehow always ended in an argument or misunderstanding. He did not know why that was—other than that Oliver Valance's magic worked differently from anyone else's—but he had accepted it as one of the many mysteries of life.

"I doubt Oliver cares much for astronomical magic, anyway," Peregrine's mother pointed out. The dowager Lady Carrington lay on a chaise longue, supposedly napping, but since she kept jumping into their conversation, her rest could not precisely be called sleep.

Peregrine liked being precise in his wording.

"He is not particularly interested in astronomical magic, no," Peregrine said regretfully. "He is too busy perfecting a system of runes for written sorcery." A task like that would probably take the rest of Valance's life, and though it was theoretically fascinating, it would be of little use to the general public. Peregrine had never met another sorcerer who worked magic by writing words rather than speaking them—or, in the case of the one deaf sorcerer he had met—signing them.

But if there was one sorcerer like Valance in the world, there might be more waiting to be discovered. Perhaps Valance's system of runes would someday help other magicians.

"Well, what about your friend Mr. Anderson—" Hannah began.

Peregrine sighed. He had considered asking Ned Anderson for help, but Ned seemed less reliable these days. Last year at this time, Ned had been obsessed with weather magic. He'd been trying to make enchanted barometers that could predict future changes in air pressure. He'd hoped to sell them to the navy once he'd perfected the enchantment.

Over the summer, though, Ned fell ill, and it had been a long time before anyone had seen him in London. When Peregrine next encountered Ned, he asked about the barometer, Ned had seemed confused. He'd acted as if he'd never heard of the project that had obsessed him only six months before.

Peregrine did not know what to make of Ned's forgetfulness, but he worried Ned would be an unreliable partner. He would rather find someone with more focus. Before Peregrine could explain any of that to his sister, though, the door opened, and someone—two someones, rather—entered the morning room unannounced. One of the visitors was a tall, broadly built, curly-haired young man who needed no introduction. Peregrine could hardly fail to recognize Oliver Valance. Not only had they grown up next door to each other, but Valance had been his housemate for nearly three years. The second visitor, though, was a stranger.

"Oliver!" Lady Carrington sat up and beamed, seeming neither to know nor care that the mobcap on her head sat askew. "What a pleasant surprise."

Peregrine ignored his friend in order to study Valance's companion. At first glance, the stranger appeared to be a young man of medium height and build, with hair of a brown color some-times described as "mousy," though in fact real mice were usually darker in color.

But that appearance was the work of a glamour. Better than most magicians at detecting magic, Peregrine could see the spell as a web of faint golden lines surrounding the stranger. *Interesting.* The last time Valance had used that spell, it had been to disguise Honora Grantly (now Lady Valance) as a young man so she could flee Belmont Court undetected.

When Peregrine peered beneath the disguise spell, he saw the stranger as a slender young man with close-cropped black curls. His hair was darker and his real eye color was much lighter than the appearance created by the spell, but his height and build remained the same.

Odd. What was the point of using a disguise spell if it changed the subject's appearance so little? One could just as easily have disguised the stranger by making him don a cap and a pair of dark glasses.

As Peregrine rose to his feet to greet the guests, he also stud-ied the way the stranger moved, listened to the way the stranger spoke, and came to some unexpected conclusions. "Valance, why is the young lady traveling with you glamoured to look like a young man? This seems to have become a habit with you, and I must say it is a strange habit."

Valance responded only with a glare. Probably he meant to convey whole paragraphs of meaning in a single look, but Peregrine had never mastered the art of such nonverbal commu-nication, so he simply ignored it.

"My lady, Hannah, Peregrine, may I present Theo Hart? Or Cora Hart, whichever the case may be?" Valance looked towards the young stranger and raised his eyebrows.

"I suppose now that I am here, it might as well be Cora," the stranger said. "Most of the time I behave like a young lady. In theory, anyway."

Miss Hart took a scrap of paper out of her pocket and tossed it into the waste bin, breaking the glamour Valance had cast on her. The paper landed neatly in the center of the basket, Peregrine noted; she had good aim. She also managed to curtsey properly, despite wearing breeches. Had she practiced that, or did such grace come naturally to her?

The most interesting thing about Miss Hart, Peregrine decided, was the color of her eyes. They very nearly matched the waistcoat she wore, suggesting she had dressed with care. More importantly, that unique blend of blue and green was almost identical to the color of Lady Valance's eyes. Until now, the former Miss Grantly was the only person Peregrine had encountered with that bright, distinctive eye color.

That made two ways in which "Cora Hart" resembled Valance's wife. Clearly, she deserved closer attention.

But Lady Carrington, apparently wanting a chance to talk to Valance and his guest alone, shooed Peregrine and Hannah out of the room on the flimsiest of pretexts. Peregrine had to wait until dinner for a chance to further observe Miss Hart. He was curious to see how she would dress for dinner. Did she always wear men's clothing, and if so, didn't other people think that odd? There were so many things that people considered odd. There seemed to be only a tiny margin of socially acceptable behavior, and anything that fell outside the margin was viewed with suspicion, derision, or fear.

Peregrine was almost a little disappointed when Miss Hart chose not to step across the margin into peculiarity. She came down to dinner wearing a white muslin dress trimmed with pink, and she looked surprisingly girlish. A simple locket hung from a matching pink ribbon about her neck, and her hair was unornamented. He supposed hair that short didn't need jeweled hair pins, did it? It would hardly need arranging at all. Quite practical, really!

Peregrine had a good view of Miss Hart, because he sat right across from her. The Carrington family rarely followed formal dining etiquette. Instead of requiring people to talk only to those seated next to them, conversation at the dinner table was general. This meant that Peregrine had a chance to ask Miss Hart questions. Her answers, though, were always slightly evasive without ever being rude. As a result, he learned very little over the course of the meal.

He changed tactics after dinner, trying to get answers from Valance instead. Unfortunately, Valance also evaded or ignored all of Peregrine's questions. Unlike Miss Hart, Valance was not very subtle about it. He grew visibly uncomfortable over the course of Peregrine's interrogation. Did he realize how much his omissions and evasions gave away? If he had simply answered directly and honestly, Peregrine might have accepted the rather thin cover story Valance presented.

Well, maybe. The story did not make that much sense. Supposedly, Miss Hart needed a place to stay because her guardian's ill health prevented her from staying at her home in Tunbridge Wells. But if that had been the truth, there would have been no reason for Valance to avoid discussing Miss Hart's family or education.

Besides, if all Miss Hart needed was a place to stay, she could have stayed with the Valances, in their London townhouse. Lady Valance would have been an adequate chaperone. He granted that the presence of Valance's mother might make the townhouse a little crowded. But in that case, why not send Miss Hart to stay at Valance's own estate? Why send her to stay at Carrington Abbey?

AFTER PEREGRINE HAD mined his friend's conversation for all the clues he could find, he moved to a more direct approach. When Hannah went to fetch something from the library, he took her seat so he could question Miss Hart himself.

"Lord Valance tells me you are a sorceress," he began without preamble. "Who was your teacher?"

She looked him in the eyes and smiled. "Oh, my father taught me. He was only a moderately powerful sorcerer, but a fairly good scholar. You would not have heard of him, though. He rarely came to London."

Peregrine had no idea whether that was the truth. It certainly *sounded* plausible. And Miss Hart had answered him without hesitation, giving no indication that she was trying to hide anything. True, he had never heard of any magical scholar by the name of "Hart." But every county in England contained at least a handful of well-trained magicians. Most of those country magicians lived quiet lives without ever making waves in the magical world. Peregrine could not have heard of all of them. It was possible that everything she said was true.

Even so, he remained skeptical. For one thing, Lady Valance's father had also been a sorcerer and scholar of good reputation. The late Sir Isaac Grantly had published articles on his theoretical work from time to time, but he rarely came to London. Peregrine had met him only once, so far as he could recall. All those details meshed very well with what Miss Hart said about *her* father. Was that supposed to be another coincidence?

When questions about Miss Hart's family proved unproductive, Peregrine tried a different angle. "Do you often dress as a man?"

She laughed—not a high pitched, affected giggle like some girls fresh out of the schoolroom, but a soft, genuine-sounding chuckle. "Not *very* often," she told him. "But I have done it a few times before. There are things that are easier to do when people think you are a boy. And really, pantaloons and trousers are sometimes more practical than skirts."

Miss Hart glanced down at her muslin gown and pulled a wry smile. "This gown is a lovely color, and sometimes I do like feeling pretty. But I would never be able to climb a tree in something like this." Then she grimaced. "Not that I was ever allowed to climb trees, but what my . . . my aunt doesn't know won't hurt her."

Peregrine sat up straighter. He'd caught the slight stumble in her speech. He did not know what she meant to say before substituting the word "aunt," but he felt very certain that it *was* a substitution for something else. She did not really live with her aunt, then? At least, her aunt was not the person who scolded her for climbing trees.

"Is something wrong?" Miss Hart furrowed her brow.

For a startling moment, she displayed the look of adorable feminine confusion Peregrine associated with flirtatious debutantes on the hunt for a husband. Such coquetry both puzzled and frustrated him. He preferred when people were more direct.

He decided then and there that he preferred Miss Hart as she had been when he met her this afternoon, dressed as a boy and acting not the least bit concerned about the supposed impropriety of her garments. If nothing else, her trousers had done a remarkable job of showing off her legs and derriere.

"Mr. Carrington?" she prompted, her frown deepening.

He realized she was waiting for him to answer. Right. Most people used words to communicate. They did not just sit in silence, thinking to themselves. But he could hardly tell their guest that he had been thinking about her shapely buttocks.

"Um. . ." Peregrine grasped for the first thing he could think of that wasn't wildly inappropriate. "I was just thinking that the waistcoat you wore this afternoon flattered you. It brought out the blue in your eyes."

That must have been a good answer, because Miss Hart smiled, revealing that she had dimples on both cheeks. He hadn't noticed that before.

"Oh, thank you. That was why I borrowed that particular waistcoat. It looks much better on me than it ever did on Tom."

"Who is Tom? Your brother?" If so, that could be another clue to her real identity.

Miss Hart shook her head. "No, he's just a friend."

"Just a friend, or actually a sweetheart whom you are pretending is a friend because you are not officially betrothed?" Oh, God, he wasn't supposed to say that, was he?

She did not look embarrassed or offended, but he could not

be certain of that. He had never been particularly good at guessing what other people were thinking.

"Just a friend," she said. "*I'm* not the one he's sweet on. But I like that waistcoat, too. In fact, I think the next time I go to London, I will wear that outfit so I can watch a dogfight or a badger drawing. Respectable young ladies don't go to those sorts of things, but someone who looks like a schoolboy playing hooky could get away with it, don't you think?"

Peregrine frowned. He had been to a dogfight only once, but he deeply regretted it. "I must advise against that," he warned. "Those events are very cruel to animals."

Miss Hart's face fell. Eager to staunch her disappointment, he continued: "If you like, I will take you to a boxing match instead. There is just as much bloodshed, but everyone agrees to be injured, so it is more ethical."

As soon as the words left his mouth, panic set in. A gentleman could not invite a young lady to a boxing match. But perhaps it did not count as improper if the young lady were disguised as gentleman? Never having been in this situation before, he had no idea what rules applied.

Her face brightened. "Oh, that would be lovely! But first, I will have to get a hat that fits properly and a pair of men's boots. I don't think my outfit looked quite right with half boots. I would like a pair of Hessian boots."

They both looked down at her feet, currently clad in a pair of black slippers. It was true that ladies' footwear looked very different from the boots gentlemen wore. Peregrine was rather surprised that her half boots had fooled anyone. Perhaps that was why she'd had Valance use a disguise spell.

"You would look smashing in Hessian boots," Peregrine said. She certainly had the legs to pull that look off. Probably she was used to walking a good deal. Perhaps while she was here, he should show her about the park? There were plenty of good walking paths.

She looked up at him and smiled that dimpled grin again.

"Wouldn't I just!"

Was she . . . flirting with him? He did not want to assume that she was. Maybe she was just being friendly. And even if she were flirting, she might be doing it for whatever inscrutable reasons inspired young ladies to coquette with young gentlemen whom they did not actually like. That possibility bothered him a good deal.

Whoever their guest really was, Peregrine hoped her smiles were not merely part of her act as "Cora Hart." And, though it could not possibly be any of his business, he hoped that "Tom" really was her friend rather than her sweetheart.

CHAPTER THREE

March, 1817

FOR ONCE, DORA remembered to bring a blanket to protect her clothing from the ground. She spread the blanket on the lawn near Carrington Abbey's landscaped wilderness, positioning herself to catch a patch of sunshine. On such a windy day, she welcomed the warmth from the occasional sunbeam, because the afternoon breeze still carried a nip.

Today, though, the cold only bothered her a little. She had dressed warmly this morning, wearing a woolen topcoat over a waistcoat and linen shirt. Her half boots kept her feet warm even though she had splashed through mud puddles to reach this solitary nook. The less said about the state of her trousers, though, the better. They were rather the worse for her ramble through the wilderness.

Muddy or not, these clothes were far more practical than a walking dress. It did not seem fair that only men were allowed to wear them. If she ran the world, Dora mused, people would be allowed to wear whatever clothing best suited their activities. Ribbons and lace and pretty gowns all had their place, but so did boots, trousers, and colorful waistcoats.

When she heard another pair of booted feet splashing through a nearby puddle, she looked up apprehensively. She had lived at Carrington Abbey for over three weeks, and she liked all of the inhabitants. Still, some part of her expected a scolding every time she did something not befitting a proper young lady— as if she expected Lady Grantly to pop up out of nowhere merely to rebuke her for wearing trousers.

But as soon as she recognized the young man approaching her, she relaxed. "Mr. Carrington," she called. "I have been looking over the notes you loaned me." She tapped the leather-bound notebook before her. "I believe you are right. I can see several places where sorcery might support the enchantment, reducing the strain on the wizard or witch who casts the primary spell. I've made a few notes about that, if you'd like to see." She had, in fact, spent a good deal of time thinking about what kind of spells might help with Mr. Peregrine Carrington's so-called meteorite trap.

"Oh, good. You can show me that in a moment." He flung himself down on the blanket, just inches away from her. A lock of light-brown hair fell over one of his eyes. He pushed it out of the way and smiled at her. Her heart promptly skipped a beat.

Now *that* was odd. Dora had only been out of the school-room for a year, but she had already spent hours flirting with young gentlemen. Some of those gentlemen had been swoon-worthily handsome, but she could not remember any of them inciting literal heart palpitations.

"I would like to look at your notes, but I have a letter to give you first. At least," he qualified, "I believe it is for you, though it is not addressed to Cora Hart."

Her whole body stiffened. At Carrington Abbey, the only people who knew her true identity were Peregrine's mother and his older brother, Sir Roderick. Outside of the Abbey, only Honora and her husband were supposed to know her whereabouts. But they also knew the alias she was using, so why would they write to her under a different name?

"Who is it from?" She kept her voice light and inquisitive, though the rapidity of her heart rate no longer had anything to do with Mr. Carrington's proximity or the very faint whiff she caught of his scent.

Well, maybe it had a *little* to do with his scent. He never seemed to wear cologne, but the warm, earthy aroma of the clove-scented soap he used lingered today, distracting her.

"It is from Lady Valance." He handed her the folded letter.

"Ah." She relaxed, though the address on the outside of the letter puzzled her. All of her sister's previous letters had been addressed to "Cora Hart," but this one was addressed to "Dora Rossini."

"I thought it might be for you, since Dora and Cora are such similar names." Young Mr. Carrington stared at her, waiting for her response. She saw no hint of anger or accusation in his face. He merely looked curious.

Even so, her mouth went dry. "The letter *is* for me," she admitted, "but I assure you, I had good reason for using a fake name. I am surprised that Honora—I mean, that Lady Valance should address this letter with my real name."

His eyes narrowed. "Who are you, then, that you call a viscountess by her first name? Her sister? Her cousin?"

Dora flinched. "What makes you say that?"

"You have a very distinctive eye color," he explained. "I noticed it the day you arrived. The only other person I have met with eyes like that is Lady Valance. I speculated that you might be a near relation of hers."

Put like that, it did seem rather obvious. Now that she thought about it, she remembered Mr. Carrington remarking on her eye color the first evening of her visit. It was, in fact, the reason she started flirting with him.

Cold disappointment washed over her. She had interpreted his remark about her eyes as a compliment. Had it merely been a deduction about her identity? If so, she might have imagined intentions on his part that did not really exist.

"Yes, I am Honora's sister. Her half sister." She drew a deep breath before telling the rest of the sordid story. "We share the same father, but I was born out of wedlock. My mother was a concert singer named Caterina Rossini, though that may have been a stage name." Her father had once implied that "Rossini" was not his late mistress's birthname, but if he knew her real name, he never told Dora.

When she lived at Grantly Manor, the truth of Dora's birth had been a secret, supposedly known only by her immediate family. Sir Isaac Grantly had never publicly owned her as his daughter. Instead, he claimed she was the daughter of a distant cousin who died and left Dora under his guardianship.

But Dora knew perfectly well that many people in their corner of Kent suspected the truth about her parentage. The sneers and sideways glances her neighbors directed at her proved as much. She could hardly fail to notice that people who were perfectly polite to her older sister might snub *her*, no matter how well she behaved in company.

Dora's looking glass and her own good sense told her that she was every bit as pretty as Honora, and she had a more gregarious personality than her bookish sister. Between her good looks and her respectable dowry, she ought to have done well in local society. Yet, young men on the hunt for a wife always looked past her. The only gentlemen who paid attention to her were those who flirted for the sake of entertainment. She enjoyed flirting back, but it stung a little that none of her flirts found her worthy of a serious courtship.

But Dora had left Grantly Manor forever. Nothing anyone could do or say would make her go back, unless she were dragged back by force—and even then, she would put up a fight. In leaving her childhood home, she intended to leave behind the pretense that she was merely Sir Isaac's ward.

She had temporarily disguised herself for her own safety, but if her disguise was no longer needed, the truth of her relationship to the Grantly family ought not be a secret, either. If there was shame attached to her birth, it was not *her* shame, but Sir Isaac's. He was the one who had chosen to break his marital vows. (Though who could blame him, with such a wife?)

Even so, she held her breath and waited for Mr. Carrington to snub her, as so many people had done in the past. She was the illegitimate daughter of a stage performer. Many people thought she did not belong in polite society, that she ought not interact on equal footing with respectable people, especially not the gentry.

The last few weeks had led Dora to hope that the Carrington family might be different in this regard. Lady Carrington seemed to cheerfully tolerate all the eccentricities of her children (and there were many) without judgment. She showed the same friendly disregard for the disreputable circumstances of Dora's birth, which had been fully explained to her upon Dora's arrival. But Dora could not be certain that all the family members shared their mother's views.

"I see." Mr. Carrington looked thoughtful, but she could not guess *what* he thought. "That explains why your last name is different from your sister's. I ought to have guessed as much. Thank you for explaining that." He smiled his most charming smile—which was very attractive indeed.

Dora blinked. It was not at all like her to be without words, but it took her a moment to gather her startled wits. "So, you knew all this time that I was lying about my identity, but you aren't angry?"

He nodded. "Why would I be angry? I must admit, I was very curious about who you were. But I assumed you had good reason to lie."

"I do. Or I did." She looked down at the still-unopened letter. "I don't suppose I could have a moment alone to read this?"

"Oh, of course. I will just look over your notes." He picked up the notebook full of semi-legible notes about the kinds of sorcery that might be incorporated into his meteorite-catching spell.

Dora broke the seal of the letter. As soon as she unfolded the paper, she saw that her sister had crossed the paper to fit more words onto a single sheet of stationery. That made it harder to read, but Dora had good eyesight, and her sister had good handwriting.

The farther she read, the more relieved she felt. When she finished reading, she folded the letter back up. A smile tugged at the corners of her mouth.

"It is good news," she reported. "The person who threatened me fled to France, so it is safe for me to come home. Back to London, I mean." That would be her home now, she supposed. Honora seemed certain that the Duke of Belmont had given up his plans for revenge. And even if he had not, Lord Valance now had leverage over him, though the letter had been vague about the precise details. With Belmont out of the picture, there was no reason why Dora could not live with her sister.

"Oh, is that good news?"

She stared at Mr. Carrington, as she struggled to parse out all the layers in his voice. "Isn't it?" Carrington Abbey was a pleasant estate, and her hosts were gracious, but she could not stay here forever. Even though she enjoyed the company of the Carrington family. Even if there was one Carrington in particular to whom she did not like saying goodbye.

"I thought perhaps you would want to stay here until we can test this new version of the enchantment," he explained. "No one in my family can work sorcery, so it would be useful to have you here during the next meteor shower."

"Ah." Dora's heart sank. For one brief moment, she'd let herself hope that he enjoyed her company as much as she did his. She should have realized that he meant nothing more than that he would have appreciated her continued assistance with his current project.

"Of course, I will miss everyone when I am gone. My visit here has been lovely." She spoke as brightly as she could, but she stared down at the blanket rather than meet Mr. Carrington's eyes.

"Did I say something wrong?" He sounded anxious now. "I do not mean to take your assistance for granted. I am very grateful for the work you have put into this spell." He tapped her notebook. "Perhaps I can write to some of the fellows at the Cambion Club and see if one of them will travel to Surrey for the next meteor shower. I really think this spell would work best if it combines wizardry and sorcery."

Dora blinked rapidly, not wanting to tear up. "I am glad I could help." The unexpected tightness of her throat made it hard to speak.

She was behaving foolishly, and she knew it. It had been ridiculous to think of Mr. Carrington in any other light than that of a colleague who could use her help. And, to be sure, it was very pleasant to be able to use her magic for such an unusual enchantment. Dora did love a challenge. She hadn't had so much fun working magic with someone since her father died.

"Of course, I will see you again when I come back to London," he continued. "I believe I promised to take you to a boxing match, did I not?"

She drew a deep breath before she looked him in the eyes. Time to be brave! "You did say that, but I will not hold you to so ridiculous a promise."

Mr. Carrington probably had no desire to attend a boxing match with her, particularly since she would have to pose as a boy again to do so. She knew nothing about boxing, but she felt fairly certain that women of the gentry were not supposed to attend matches, whether they wore pantaloons or skirts.

"Oh, would you rather do something else? I know driving in Hyde Park is the customary thing to do with the lady one is courting, but I don't know how to drive a team." His face brightened. "I can ride, though. We could ride on Rotten Row if you like. Er, if you know how to ride, I mean?"

This time, Dora's heart did not just skip: it somersaulted. *The lady one is courting*, he said. There could be no misunderstanding *that*.

"I do know how to ride," she replied. "I would like that very much."

"Then we shall do that." It might have been her imagination, but she thought she could *see* the tension leaving his lean frame. Certainly, he looked far more at his ease.

The sun peeked out from behind a cloud, and the whole day

brightened. Suddenly, everything seemed possible. "Maybe I should write to my sister and see if I can stay here until the meteor shower," Dora suggested. "That way you would not have to find another sorcerer to assist you."

"Oh, that would be splendid!" That winsome smile broke across his face again, and his bright eyes crinkled at the corners.

This time, Dora smiled back.

CHAPTER FOUR

April, 1817

PEREGRINE SURVEYED THE east pasture of the farm that fed Carrington Abbey. The dairy cows who usually grazed here had all been moved to a different pasture so that they would not disturb his work area. Or maybe it would be more accurate to say that they'd been moved so his work would not harm them. Roderick was more likely to be concerned about the cows than about Peregrine's spell.

One of the groundskeeper's assistants had stripped a wide swath of grass, just as Peregrine had requested. He did not believe falling stars were incendiary, but Roderick had expressed concerns about the possibility of a fire. That was why Peregrine's enchantment was to be cast here, well away from trees or buildings.

So far as he could tell, everything was as ready as it could be. Tomorrow, he would lay out lines of salt and colored sand to make a giant pentacle. He would work the base of the enchantment with wizardry, and Dora would layer sorcery over that. They had tested the spell structure more than once, and it was good as they could make it. The only thing left to worry about was the meteorite itself. If the Lyrid meteor shower did not happen as predicted, all their work would be for naught.

But Peregrine trusted the astronomical magic that predicted the shower would occur tomorrow night. Tomorrow, then, he would finally have a chance to use the spell he'd been developing since a chance sight of last November's Leonids first sparked his dream of catching a falling star. Tomorrow, he would know whether the current enchantment had merit, or if he needed to go back to the drawing board and retheorize the whole project.

And after that? Things would change a good deal. In a few days, Dora would go back to London with her sister and her brother-in-law. Peregrine would return to London himself next week, but he would no longer have Dora under the same roof with him. He would no longer have the freedom to walk or talk with her unchaperoned. Behavior that his own family might wink at would be censured by upper-class London society.

This might be his best chance to come to an understanding with Dora, then. Assuming she liked him as much as he liked her. He thought she had shown signs of interest—but what if he was wrong?

Peregrine had no prior experience of courtship. In the past, he'd been content to admire young ladies from afar, telling himself that courtship and flirtation took time that he would rather spend on his magical studies. On some level, he feared he was too awkward, too bookish, or too odd to appeal to the objects of his admiration, and the potential benefits did not seem worth the risk of humiliation.

Other men in his situation might have felt lonely, but Peregrine had a large, affectionate family, a handful of close friends, and the camaraderie of his club. As for his physical desires, he'd found ample consolation in the company of women of easy virtue. They overlooked his awkwardness and eccentricity so long as he treated them politely and paid them well. Until now, such interactions had contented him.

But Dora Rossini was the daughter of a baronet. She might have been born on the wrong side of the blanket, but she had been educated and reared as a gentlewoman. Anyone could see that—at least, when she chose to act like a young lady.

The fact that she did not always choose to behave with propriety only increased her appeal in Peregrine's eyes. He often felt that social rules made little sense, so it was a pleasure to find in

Dora a kindred spirit—someone willing to ignore arbitrary rules in favor of acting logically. It was not often that a girl like that crossed one's path. And he was no longer content to admire her from afar.

Given that Dora planned to leave Carrington Abbey in a matter of days, it might be wisest to make his proposals now. But he worried that any sort of declaration on his part would seem premature. Dora might not think two months was enough time in which to decide to spend one's life with a person. *He* had no doubts, but he had no idea what she thought of him. Maybe she would be shocked if he proposed to her. Perhaps he would succeed in nothing more than making their last days together horrifically awkward. How was he to know?

He strode back through the pasture, then through the wilderness that surrounded the formal gardens. Springtime at the Abbey was always beautiful, but today the sun shone brighter than usual, and the air smelled sweeter.

On a normal day, Peregrine might have lingered in the flower gardens to see if anything new was in bloom. Today, his mind was so occupied that he did not take time to smell the flowers, either literally or figuratively.

He entered the house through the library doors, then walked down the hall to the study. He was in luck: The door had been cracked open, indicating that his older brother did not mind being disturbed. Even so, he tapped at the door and politely waited for permission to enter, rather than simply barging in the way he'd often done as a child.

"Ah, Peregrine!" Roderick looked up from the letter he was writing. Stacks of correspondence on both sides of his desk suggested he'd been at this for a while. "I expected you to be working on your wizardry." He pointed to the chair facing his desk, and Peregrine obediently took a seat.

"Not wizardry alone," Peregrine corrected. "An enchantment that employs both wizardry and sorcery—"

Before he could say more, Roderick silenced him with a wave

of his hand. "My apologies. You know how little I know about magic." Or, his tone implied, how little he cared about the details of the spell.

Peregrine closed his mouth and nodded. It was not Roderick's fault he had inherited no magical gift from either of his parents. Though magical talent was heritable, it did not follow the law of primogeniture. There was no predicting whether or not the children of a magician would inherit their parents' gifts. Magical abilities weren't always evenly distributed among siblings, and they sometimes skipped whole generations.

"In any case," Peregrine concluded, "there is nothing more to be done at the moment. I wished to speak to you about something else entirely." He fell silent, not certain how to introduce the topic. He had never before discussed women with Roderick.

"Yes?" Roderick prompted.

"How did you decide when to propose to Amelia?" Peregrine asked.

Roderick's eyes widened. "What does that have to do with anything?"

Peregrine shrugged, feeling sheepish. "I just wondered. It did not take you long to court her, and I wondered how you knew when she would accept your suit."

Roderick snorted. "I did *not* know that she would accept my suit. I had, in fact, no idea how she felt about me. But someone told me that Lord Harvey planned to propose to her, and I wanted to beat him to it." His rueful grin broadened into a full smile. "Fortunately, she preferred me."

"Oh. I see." That was interesting, but not particularly helpful for Peregrine's situation. It was not as if he had a rival for Dora's hand.

At least, not a local rival. Dora had little chance to meet eligible bachelors here, not that there were many in rural Surrey. Due to Amelia's rough pregnancy, the Carrington family did little entertaining these days. They'd only had guests to dine a handful of times since Dora arrived.

But all that might change when Dora went back to London. Valance circulated in society far more than Peregrine did, and he would probably introduce his sister-in-law to any number of eligible bachelors. Some of them would be wealthier, better looking, or possessing of greater address than Peregrine.

"Thank you for answering my question." He got to his feet, intending to leave.

"Wait a moment." Roderick narrowed his eyes, fixing Peregrine with a keen stare. "Are you planning on declaring yourself to Miss Rossini before she leaves?"

"I didn't say anything about Miss Rossini!" he protested.

To his dismay, his older brother chuckled. "Who else could you be talking about, Perry? I assumed it was merely a matter of time."

Peregrine's mouth fell open a fraction. "You knew?"

"That you were courting Miss Rossini? Of course. We all knew! In fact, Hannah and Amelia have a wager going as to how soon you will propose. It sounds as if Hannah will win." Roderick smiled. "If you are worried about whether you have our approval, you need not be," he assured Peregrine. "I suppose it is not a brilliant match from a worldly perspective, but Miss Rossini seems to suit you quite well, and I know Mother is already fond of her."

Peregrine slowly sank back into his chair, shocked to find that something he had never spoken about to anyone was so widely known. And, apparently, widely discussed. Not to mention being the subject of a wager between his sister-in-law and his younger sister. Just how much had they wagered on it, anyway?

Roderick's face fell into more serious lines. "Some people would say that three-and-twenty is a little young to marry, but I must say it is a relief to me to see you settled. Given Amelia's poor health, the child she is carrying will likely be our last, and if it is another girl—well, there is nothing *wrong* with Cousin Andrew, but he is not the man that I would choose to inherit the Abbey. It will be good to have the succession secured."

Peregrine shook his head, feeling faintly sick. He could not imagine taking Roderick's place as baronet. Surely that would never happen? Besides, Roderick seemed to be jumping to unwarranted conclusions.

"I have no idea whether Miss Rossini will favor my suit," Peregrine warned his brother.

To his surprise, Roderick chuckled again. "If she does not favor your suit, she is a very good actress. I am no mind reader, but I suspect she is rather fond of you."

"You think so?" His heart bounded with hope, but he did his best to rein it in. Dora did seem to enjoy his company, but it did not necessarily follow that she wanted to marry him. There was a world of difference between collaborating on a spell and spending a lifetime together.

"Yes," Roderick said dryly, "and if you don't believe me, you can go and ask anyone else in the family."

"Oh." Peregrine could think of nothing else to say, so he smiled rather shakily and made his exit.

Though it was theoretically possible that the entire Carrington family was mistaken about Dora's affections, it did not seem plausible. Perhaps he need not worry about his prospects after all. Feeling slightly relieved, he put the question aside and went up to the laboratory to check his magical supplies one last time.

ON THE BIG day, he spent the better part of the morning drawing the pentacle and laying down the groundwork for the spell. In the afternoon, Dora joined him to work the sorcery that would reinforce and strengthen his magic. By the time he went to dress for dinner, everything was ready. All it would take was a single invocation to activate the whole enchantment. They would wait until nightfall to do that, to avoid wasting power.

And, Peregrine decided, he would wait until tomorrow to

declare his affections. Dora was not going to leave immediately, so there would be time. He would be able to concentrate on his confession once tonight's meteor shower ended. Just now, his mind was full of incantations, inscriptions, the position of the constellations above Carrington Abbey, and the trajectory the falling stars might take.

Oliver Valance and his wife, Honora, arrived shortly before dinner. Though they both professed curiosity about Peregrine's spell, it quickly became clear that Honora was most interested in catching up with her sister, whom she had not seen for weeks. After dinner, the Grantly sisters closeted themselves in a corner of the drawing room to talk together.

Peregrine, who had grown used to taking the space by Dora's side, glanced wistfully across the room at them. Only for a moment, though. Then he turned to Valance, eager to explain what would happen during tonight's meteor shower. It couldn't hurt to have another sorcerer on hand.

Once full darkness fell over the estate, most of the Carringtons and both of the Valances tromped out to the east pasture, bundled up in coats and pelisses. Dora had wisely changed her dinner dress for a set of men's clothing, including a new pair of Hessian boots.

Busy as he was, Peregrine still took a moment to admire her. Boots and tight pantaloons showed off her legs far more than a loose skirt would have done. Why didn't more women dress this way? Skirts concealed so many of the lines and curves that made women's bodies alluring.

Then again, he discovered, a greatcoat also hid a good deal of a woman's body. Once Dora shrugged on one of Cosmo's old coats, she no longer presented such a distracting sight. Perhaps that was just as well, given that they had work to do.

The night was surprisingly cool for mid-April. A stiff breeze blew all the clouds out of the sky, but it also chilled everyone who'd failed to dress warmly. Some of the family members gathered in the pasture seemed inured to the chill, but Susan

Taylor shivered with cold as she read by the glow of a witchlight.

Peregrine's older sister fussed over Susan, who caught chest colds easily and tended to cough for far longer than anyone else. While Abigail tucked a shawl about her companion, Valance scribbled one of his written sorceries on a scrap of paper. Peregrine squinted at it until he recognized the pattern of magic: a warming spell to keep Susan from catching a chill.

Being a sorcerer, Valance could more easily work magic on the fly than any of the Carrington magicians, who required *materia magica* for their work. But, since Peregrine was capable of working more complicated and more powerful magic than Valance, he did not begrudge his friend this advantage. He did wish that he'd thought to work some magic to keep the field warm, though. He ought to have anticipated that need.

He wished that even more an hour later, when they were all still waiting—some more patiently than others—for one of the shooting stars to pass through the portion of the sky above the meteorite trap. Perhaps he ought to have made the pentacle even wider, so as to increase the chances of catching one of the meteors passing so far overhead. If necessary, he would try again during the next meteor shower, but he hoped—

Suddenly, Peregrine felt the spell snap into action. He had to close his eyes against the blaze of light that suddenly lit up the pasture. He had not expected anything quite this dramatic. Was that a physical effect of the meteor crashing, or merely some kind of magical side effect of the spell itself? Probably the latter, but he could not be certain. He'd have to investigate further.

Peregrine had been prepared for the thump as the speeding rock landed in the center of the pentacle, but he realized, too late, that he had not warned everyone else. He heard startled exclamations as the ground rolled beneath people's feet, throwing everyone off-balance.

Someone quickly summoned a witchlight to illuminate the pasture. By its glow, Peregrine saw that Dora stood squarely on her own two feet, no worse for the bump. Others had not fared so well. Lady Valance would have tumbled to the ground if her husband had not caught her. Abigail held Lady Carrington's arm, steadying her. Roderick had kept his footing, but he looked shaken. Susan, who had sensibly remained in her chair the whole time, looked entirely unaffected.

After ascertaining that no one had taken a fall, Peregrine turned back to Dora. When her eyes met his, a broad grin split her face. The sight of her dimpled smile sent Peregrine's heart fluttering.

"Peregrine, we did it!" She bounded towards him and flung her arms about him.

Next thing he knew, Peregrine was caught in a tight embrace. Dora was a few inches shorter than him, and hatless, so her mop of curls brushed against his face. She smelled faintly of herbs: some cosmetic, some magical.

Startled into speechlessness, Peregrine froze. He had not expected *this*. But he certainly did not mind. He'd been longing to have Dora in his arms for weeks. There was something else he'd wanted to do, too, and this seemed the perfect time to do it. He wrapped his arms around her, and when she looked up at him, he pressed his lips lightly against hers.

She must not have minded, because she enthusiastically kissed him back.

A soft murmur passed through the friends and family gathered around them, but no one seemed particularly dismayed. Predictably, the only objection came from Roderick.

"Peregrine," his brother scolded, "it is generally considered advisable to receive permission to marry a girl before you kiss her. You ought to have waited until after you spoke to Miss Rossini's guardian to do that."

Peregrine knew his brother well enough to tell that Roderick was not angry. Most likely he scolded only because he thought he ought to do so. He sometimes took his responsibilities as head of the family a little too seriously.

"That will be difficult," Lady Valance pointed out, "given that we are not on good terms with the rest of the Grantly family at the moment."

Dora wrinkled her nose in distaste. "As if I care what Lady Grantly and Uncle Robert think!" she whispered to Peregrine.

He tightened his grip on her. Dora rarely spoke about Lady Grantly or her uncle, but what little he had heard suggested they were unfit to be her guardians. He did not particularly care about their opinions, either, and he hated the fact that they had legal power over Dora. But there were ways around that. . .

"Oh, we can simply run off to Scotland to marry," he suggested. North of the border, Dora would not need her guardians' permission to marry. Nor would they have to wait to call the banns. The long distance was the only inconvenience.

Some of his family looked shocked at his suggestion, but Dora merely grinned up at him before standing on her toes to brush a kiss against his cheek. Peregrine took that to be a sign of assent, which meant he could check two things off his list of things to do. Not only was he betrothed, but the betrothal had been announced to (almost) his entire family. Who knew it could be so easy?

With that settled, he could turn his mind back his spell. It had worked! He paused briefly to savor that fact. This was the most complicated piece of magic he'd ever done, and he hadn't been sure the enchantment would be strong enough to pull a meteor shooting across the heavens all the way down to earth. Some of the other magicians in the Cambion Club had laughed at him for thinking such a thing was even possible.

And those who were too polite to laugh in his face had nevertheless exchanged the skeptical looks he'd seen his entire life when he tried to explain one of his theories. He interpreted that look to mean "Just another one of Carrington's wild ideas," and he deeply resented it.

Well, they would laugh no more. This idea, at least, could no longer be dismissed as the pipe dream of an absent-minded scholar.

Warmth flooded out from his chest. He'd won the hand of the girl of his heart and he'd just achieved the kind of success most magicians only dreamed of. Everything was coming together perfectly tonight, almost as if the meteor shower had brought him good fortune.

But, he reminded himself, he still had work to do. Time to get back to it. Now that he knew the spell worked, he wanted to present it to the annual spring meeting of the Society of Astronomical Magicians. That gave him less than a month to draft the paper he would read. His matrimonial plans would have to wait.

CHAPTER FIVE

May, 1817

"WHAT DO YOU mean, they won't consent to the marriage?" Dora demanded. "What grounds do they have to refuse?" She stiffened with anger. Quite an accomplishment, actually, because the hard wooden dining room chair forced her to sit stiffly to begin with.

Lord Valance's solicitor adjusted his spectacles. Mr. Watson was a man of middle years who radiated patience and stability. But Dora had known from the moment she first looked into his eyes that he'd come bearing bad news.

"I must say that their reasons do not seem particularly persuasive," he admitted. "I probably ought not say this, but their man of law, Mr. Epps, confided in me that he was surprised that Mr. Grantly rejected a gentleman as suitable as Mr. Carrington."

A smile tugged at the corners of Dora's mouth as she thought of all the things that made Peregrine suitable. His attractive smile, his intelligence, the way he not only accepted but encouraged Dora's occasional violations of propriety, his skill at kissing. . .

Mr. Watson disrupted her daydream with hard facts. "As you may be aware, Mr. Carrington inherited an independent fortune from his great uncle, a Mr. Peregrine Howell. As a result, Mr. Carrington is quite able to support a wife and family in comfort—even, to some degree, in luxury. He owns a share of Carrington House, too, which means you would never lack a home." He peered over his spectacles. "Most younger sons cannot claim such advantages, Miss Rossini."

"Yes, I know," Dora said meekly. Clearly, *suitable* meant something quite different to Mr. Watson than it did to her. "I would have thought those details would impress my stepmother. I expected her to be happy to see me well-settled." Given Dora's illegitimacy, this was really a match beyond her expectations, though no one had been rude enough to say so.

"One would think." Mr. Watson allowed a hint of disapproval into his voice. "Particularly given that Lord Valance has known Mr. Carrington all his life and can vouch for his good character and respectability." He nodded at Valance.

For some reason, this comment seemed to embarrass Valance. He returned Mr. Watson's nod, then averted his eyes. Interesting. Did he know something disreputable about his friend? Dora made a mental note to ask some questions about that later.

"Then why does my stepmother object?" Dora had assumed Lady Grantly would be delighted to finally get her unwanted ward out of the house.

Faced with such a question, a lesser man might have quailed, but Mr. Watson met her eyes steadily. "Pardon my plain speaking, but Lady Grantly claims to have some doubts about your level of maturity, Miss Rossini. Mr. Epps conveyed that both your guardians are concerned that your running away from home indicates poor judgment and a lack of the steadiness desirable in a married woman."

"Miss Rossini ran away because her stepmother was mistreating her!" Valance argued. "The Grantlys were violating the terms of Sir Isaac's will. And it isn't as if Dora ran off and joined the circus. She went straight to her older sister—which, under, the circumstances, was a perfectly reasonable thing to do." He fairly bristled with righteous indignation. Dora found it quite touching.

"I quite agree." Mr. Watson used a soothing voice. "Lady Valance was in a position to aid her natural sibling, so it was entirely reasonable for Miss Rossini to seek her assistance. However, this argument is unlikely to sway Mr. Grantly, given that he denies mistreating Miss Rossini."

"Bullshit," Valance grumbled. He crossed his arms over his chest and leaned back in his chair, glowering impressively.

"Indeed," Mr. Watson said dryly. He pulled a thick packet of legal papers out of a well-worn leather satchel and laid them on the table. "I have looked over Sir Isaac's will very carefully. It is quite clear that sending Miss Rossini to work as a servant contradicts the terms of the will. We will most certainly use that as grounds for our appeal to Chancery."

He turned back to Dora. "I believe that is our best recourse, at least for now. The Court of Chancery has the power to grant you permission to marry, or to replace your current legal guardians. Given the explicit terms of Sir Isaac's will and the clear suitability of Mr. Carrington as a suitor, I believe we will win our case. But it will take time. Chancery is known for moving slowly."

Dora sighed. This was not the answer she'd hoped for. "They can't force me to go back to Grantly Manor, can they?" With her hands hidden under the dining room table, she was free to worry a hangnail without anyone noticing. At least, she hoped so.

Mr. Watson frowned. "They could try. Mr. Grantly and Lady Grantly are still your legal guardians, so the law would be on their side. However, taking you back by force might weaken their case in the long run, because it could undermine their claim to have only your best interests in mind."

Dora puckered her brow, not quite following this. Mr. Watson must have seen her confusion, because he promptly elaborated. "In many ways, staying with Lord and Lady Valance is ideal, because they are able to introduce you into London society. You are the perfect age to make a London come out, Miss Rossini. I doubt that the Grantlys could afford to give you one, but your sister can. It would be hard to justify taking that opportunity away from you."

"In other words," Valance said, "if they really cared about Dora's well-being, they would want her to have a Season in London. If they try to take her back, it will be clear that they do not want what is best for her."

"Precisely." Mr. Watson returned the paperwork to his bag. "That said, you will want to be on your very best behavior while in London, Miss Rossini. You will need stay above reproach, because a public scandal would lend support to your guardians' claim that you are not mature enough to marry."

"And it would raise questions about whether Honora and I are adequate guardians," Valance added.

Dora's heart sank. "Oh, I see," she said weakly. "My best behavior. Yes, that makes sense. Of course I will stay out of trouble!"

She smiled politely, hoping it looked genuine. She was fairly certain Mr. Watson would be appalled if he knew that she already had plans to infiltrate the annual meeting of the Society of Astronomical Magicians in less than a week.

DORA KNEW BETTER than to expect fame and fortune as a result of Peregrine's successful magical experiment, but she *had* expected accolades and attention—not for herself, but for him. In capturing a falling star through magic, he'd done something no other magician had ever done. Frankly, Dora thought the Society of Astronomical Magicians should bestow an award on him for accomplishing something previously thought to be impossible.

But Peregrine did not win an award. The year's Achievement Award went to a member of the Society who had invented an improved method of tracking comets using a scrying mirror, a pinch of colored salt, and a smoking brazier of herbs. Dora was baffled that this work was considered more important than Peregrine's spell. She wondered if the decision had something to do with the fact that the comet-tracking magician looked about eighty years old. Perhaps they wanted to recognize him before it was too late?

At least the members of the Society paid attention to Peregrine's presentation. After he read his paper, many audience members asked questions. In fact, the question-and-answer session devolved into a heated argument that ended only when the president of the society called a halt to the discussion, forcefully reminding everyone that other magicians needed to read their papers too, thank you very much. That part of the day was every bit as fun as Dora had hoped.

But the rest of the conference? Not quite so interesting, alas. The paper currently being read was a good example. It was about the way the phases of the moon affected magical herbs. The presenter revealed a complicated formula for determining the best time of the lunar cycle for gathering key herbs like foxglove and henbane. No doubt if Dora had been a witch who practiced medical magic, this would have been very useful information, but as a sorceress, she did not work with herbs or other magical ingredients. Instead of taking notes, she found herself doodling and yawning.

Dora stole a surreptitious glance at Peregrine. He wore his hair longer than was fashionable, merely because he did not like having his hair cut. As a result, an errant lock of hair once again wandered across his eyes. Dora's hand itched to brush it away, but she could not do that while they sat in public.

Peregrine bent over his notebook, his hand racing to take notes. Unlike Dora, he could work simple healing spells, but he rarely did so, medicine not being one of his particular interests.

Dora suspected that the notes were actually for the benefit of Abigail Carrington, who sometimes devoted both her time and her witchcraft to medical charities. Abigail most often visited an infirmary one of her friends managed in the East End, but she occasionally helped out at the Foundling Hospital that Susan supported.

Dora watched her betrothed for a moment. Then she tore a scrap of paper out of her own notebook and wrote "Going out to the gallery to stretch my legs." She folded the paper and slipped it onto Peregrine's notebook. He stopped writing and blinked in surprise. But when he read the note, he caught her eye and nodded. Dora slipped out of her chair and crept as quietly as she could to the door.

Once she stepped into the gallery, she released a sigh of relief. She tugged on her cravat, which Peregrine must've tied too tightly. Surely it wasn't supposed to be this uncomfortable? Then she sauntered down the right side of the gallery to study a display of star charts, the click of her boots on the marble floor filling the quiet space.

When she saw that she was not alone, she froze. Had she been walking like a young lady, or like a young man? There was such a difference in posture and the deportment that someone might suspect her if she did not take care to move the right way.

But the white-haired gentleman who had been studying the star chart lifted his head and smiled faintly at her in a way that suggested he saw nothing suspicious. Dora relaxed fractionally as she nodded her head in greeting. She had never seen this man before, but that was no surprise. She had only been in London for a couple of weeks, and she'd only just dipped her toes into the metaphorical waters of the Season.

She knew enough about clothing to recognize that the stranger was dressed very expensively, though the cut of his topcoat and tie of his cravat were both understated, suggesting he had no pretension to fashion. Or, given how seldom wealthy men of the *ton* dressed themselves, perhaps the conservative taste belonged to his valet.

"You look rather young for this meeting," the gentleman suggested. "Are you accompanying your father?"

Dora's throat tightened. Her father had been dead for more than two years, and even if he were alive, he would never have taken her to an event like this. He had always encouraged her study of magic, but he would never have publicly acknowledged that she inherited her magical talent from him. That would have meant admitting she was his child.

Then again, Sir Isaac wouldn't have taken his legitimate daughters with him to a professional meeting like this, either. Lady Grantly did not view intellectual attainments or scholarly advancement as ladylike. Sir Isaac had privately seen that his two eldest daughters got an education beyond the traditional feminine accomplishments, but he was unlikely to fight his wife on something that involved his daughters' public behavior.

"No," Dora said, "I am here with a friend. A Mr. Carrington." If this man was a member of the Society, he likely knew Peregrine.

And she was right. The stranger immediately looked more interested. "Would that be Mr. Peregrine Carrington or Mr. Cosmo Carrington? They are the magicians of the family, if I recall correctly."

"They are the family *wizards*, but their elder sister is a magician, too." It was not good manners to rebuke a stranger, but Abigail Carrington was a powerful witch, and she most certainly deserved to be ranked among the family magicians. "But Cosmo is not interested in astronomy. I am here with Peregrine."

Too late, she realized that she ought not have used their first names so casually. Especially as she had not, in fact, ever met Cosmo. But after living with the Carrington family for two months, she was used to talking about all the siblings as familiarly as if she had known them all her life.

The stranger nodded. "That was a most impressive piece of magic Mr. Peregrine developed. Sir John would be proud of him."

Never having met Sir John Carrington, Dora could only take the stranger's word for that. "The whole family was proud of him for catching the meteorite." Then, though she knew she was bragging, she added: "I helped him cast the enchantment, since I am a sorcerer. That is why he sponsored my induction into the society."

Naturally, her application had omitted some details about her identity, such as the fact that her given name was *Theodora* rather than *Theodore*.

The gentleman raised his eyebrows, looking suitably impressed. "You are to be congratulated too, then. You look a little young to be joining any gentlemen's clubs yet, but when you do, you ought to consider joining the Cambion Club. You will meet many of the best magicians in London there."

"Oh, I know." Dora nearly told him that her father had been a member. But she could not reveal that Sir Isaac Grantly was her father, because everyone knew that Sir Isaac's only son was a child of ten years. Instead, she said "Mr. Carrington is a member, too, of course. So is Lord Valance."

"Ah, yes. Naturally, if you know the Carringtons, you would know the Valances too," the stranger agreed, as if this were a foregone conclusion. Perhaps it was, given that the Carringtons tended to treat Lord Valance as part of the family. "You ought to come to our dinner party next Thursday." He reached into his waistcoat pocket and pulled out a card. "I will take the liberty of introducing myself, since we have mutual acquaintances. I am Kellway."

"Oh." It was rare for anything to silence Dora, but it took her a moment to absorb this revelation. She had been speaking to the President of the Cambion Club, a man who had considerable influence in London's magical community. Perhaps more importantly, Peregrine admired him, which said a good deal about his character and abilities. Peregrine never admired people merely on account of their rank or wealth.

"I haven't got a card yet," she said apologetically, "but I am Theo Rossini."

She steeled herself for the signs of disdain that sometimes accompanied the revelation of her Italian surname. The British often held unflattering stereotypes about people from other countries. French, Italian, or German *émigrés* from distinguished or noble families might be welcomed and treated with respect, but not every Italian exile had the good fortune of Gabriele Rossetti or Gaetano Polidori.

But Lord Kellway did not sneer or flinch. He looked intrigued. "Any relationship to Rafaele Rossini? The mage?"

"Not that I'm aware." For all she knew, Rafaele Rossini could have been her uncle or cousin. She rather doubted that, though. A mage of whom Lord Kellway spoke respectfully probably did not have a near relation who had earned her bread as a concert singer and courtesan.

"I do not have many living relatives from that side of the family," Dora added. She needed to be careful about her lies on this subject, since she knew nothing about her mother's family. Under the circumstances, changing the subject seemed wise. "Are you a student of astronomy, then?" She expected him to say 'Yes,' because why else would he be attending this meeting?

But Lord Kellway surprised her by shaking his head. "No, I am not a member of this society. My interest lies in an entirely different direction. I study geological magic."

Dora quickly sorted through a range of possible responses. "What brings you here, then?" seemed like a safe enough question.

He hesitated before answering. "I suppose I am here in the capacity of an observer. A friend of mine asked me to investigate one of our club members who is suspected of ungentlemanly conduct. The person in question is present at this meeting." He lowered his eyebrows and turned down the corners of his mouth, giving Dora the impression that "ungentlemanly" might be a euphemism for some stronger term of condemnation.

This was the most intriguing thing Dora had heard for the last few hours. A magician engaging in "ungentlemanly conduct" seemed far more interesting than a method for determining the best phase of the moon in which to harvest plants. Lord Kellway's involvement puzzled her, too. She knew very little of gentlemen's clubs, but she'd never heard that presiding over such a club involved the art of detection.

She lost the opportunity to ask any further questions about Lord Kellway's investigation when the door to the lecture room opened up. A throng of soberly dressed gentlemen, most of them of advanced years, flooded into the gallery. Dora stepped closer to the wall so as not to be swept up in the flood. Lord Kellway was swarmed by people wanting to exchange greetings. She was not surprised to see him borne away by a cluster of acquaintances, leaving her alone.

Where was Peregrine? Dora struggled to peer through the crowd. She was tall for a woman, but most of the gentlemen here were taller than her, and they blocked her view. Gradually, though, the flood thinned to a trickle, and the murmur of voices fell silent. Then the gallery stood empty.

A pang twisted her heart. Could he have left without her? Had he gotten so absorbed in his thoughts that he had forgotten her? It was not beyond the realm of possibility. When Peregrine was well into his work, he thought of nothing else.

Dora uneasily wondered whether she remembered the way back from Bedford Street to Curzon Street. She had not thought to bring fare to hire a hack, since she was traveling with Peregrine. She had just convinced herself that she could get back quite easily if she asked directions, when she thought to look out the window. Her shoulders slumped. It had begun to rain, and she had not brought her umbrella.

She very much hoped Peregrine had not forgotten her.

CHAPTER SIX

PEREGRINE HAD NOT forgotten about his companion. Not exactly. There was a sizeable chamber of his mind devoted solely to Dora, and he never let the thought of her leave his head. It was just that when he became very deeply involved in something else, it might be some time before he glanced into that room, so to speak.

In this case, he had been about to go and look for her when he was waylaid by a short, round-faced man with steel-gray hair.

"I don't know if you remember me, Mr. Carrington," the man said, "but we were introduced at a Christmas party last year, and I believe I have seen you at the Cambion Club. I am Thomas Blithfield."

"I am sorry to say that I did not recognize you," Peregrine admitted. "I do not have a good memory for faces."

At least, he did not remember Blithfield's face. But perhaps that was because there was nothing particularly distinctive about the gentleman, apart from the even steel tone of his hair. His name, though—the name "Blithfield" did ring a very faint bell. Where had he heard that name before?

"I was most fascinated by your talk," Blithfield said. "I am new to the field of astronomical magic, though I have already learned a good deal from the Society. I wondered if you could explain to me your theory about the extraterrestrial magic found in meteorites?"

"Oh, of course!" Peregrine temporarily set aside all thoughts of Dora while he explained the hotly disputed theory that meteorites contained magical elements not found on earth. He had invented the meteorite trap primarily in order to investigate this hypothesis, though he might have to capture many more meteorites in order to either support or debunk it.

The meteorite he'd caught in April contained no detectable trace of magic, but no one knew if all shooting stars were alike. It might be that some of them contained magical elements and others did not. Much more research would have to be done, probably over a period of many years, and Peregrine hoped that magicians in other parts of the world would replicate his experiment, so as to collect more samples—

"I say," Blithfield interrupted, "this conversation has gone far over my head. I am afraid I am not scholar enough to follow you." He wiped his forehead and smiled apologetically.

"Oh, my apologies." Peregrine's shoulders drooped. He had done it again, hadn't he? He'd completely missed the signs that he'd lost his audience.

At least this happened less often than when he'd been a schoolboy. Other boys in his form had teased him mercilessly about the habit, until Valance started thrashing any student who bullied his friend. That had made school a little more tolerable.

"You need not apologize!" Mr. Blithfield reassured him. "I shall have to do more reading before I speak to you again, that is all. But I hope we can discuss the subject again sometime soon. Do you intend to make a long stay in London?"

"I plan to go back to the country about midsummer," Peregrine replied, "but I will be in town for some weeks yet."

Between the heat and the odor, no one liked London in the summer. Even if Peregrine had wanted to stay in Russell Square after the season ended, his mother would insist that he come back for at least a short visit once Cosmo was home for the Long Vacation. Lady Carrington had rather strong opinions about the importance of the family spending time together.

"Excellent. I will send you a card for one of my dinner parties."

Blithfield drifted toward the exit, and Peregrine followed him. But something niggled at the back of his mind. Wasn't there something he needed to do? Someone he needed to find? He looked back over his shoulder, wondering if he had left something in his seat. But no, his chair was empty, as was Dora's.

Oh, yes. Dora! "I beg your pardon, Mr. Blithfield, but I have just remembered that I must meet someone in the gallery. I hope to see you again soon. If you want any recommendations for further reading, you may drop me a note." He did not wait for a response before trotting out of the lecture room into the long gallery.

When he saw Dora, a jolt of relief set his heart pounding more heavily for a moment. At least, he thought it was relief. His heart often did seem to behave oddly around Dora, though. How long would that last? Would he still be bothered with palpitations after they were married, or would his heart settle back down to its usual rhythm? Maybe he should ask Valance.

"I thought I had lost you," he said once he drew within earshot.

She smiled ruefully. "I thought perhaps you had forgotten me, and I was trying to decide whether I was brave enough to walk home in the rain without an umbrella." She glanced out the nearest window and pulled a face.

"You need not walk home. We will hire a hackney coach." He offered her his arm to escort her, but she shook her head.

"I cannot take your arm when I am disguised as a boy," she whispered.

"Oh, right. Such stupid rules." Changing one's clothing did not change one's relationship to other people. Whether she dressed in trousers or in skirts, Dora was still his love.

But Peregrine did not want to cause an unnecessary scandal. Hadn't Dora specifically told him she needed to avoid becoming the subject of gossip? He most certainly did not want to do anything that would weaken the legal case against the Grantlys. He lowered his arm and did his best to pretend that he was walking beside a good friend, rather than the love of his life.

He intended to simply drop Dora off at her sister's house, but Honora invited him to stay for dinner, and then Valance wanted his opinion as to the soundness of a new spell he was working on. Between one thing and another, his conversation with Blithfield passed out of his mind.

A FEW NIGHTS later, all his attention was drawn to another new acquaintance. He came home late, thinking about possible modifications that might make the meteorite trap more efficient. The current enchantment required considerable magical power, making it impractical for most wizards. Peregrine wondered if there was a way to draw more power from the physical ingredients used in the spell, rather than relying on the personal resources of the witch or wizard who cast it.

What about adding starflower to the mix? Peregrine rarely used starflower, but Abigail kept some on hand for medicinal purposes. Most of the dry herbs were stored in the unused nursery; he decided to pop in and check the stores. He would need the flower rather than the leaves, since its rather tenuous connection to astronomy depended on the shape of the blossom.

He poked his head into the nursery and said *"Lucernam accendatur."* As a general rule, Peregrine could not work sorcery, but the traditional candle lighting spell worked for him, as it did for many wizards, because the wax of the candles fueled the spell. Some theorists claimed the spell worked because candles *wanted* to be lit, but Peregrine did not approve of ascribing human emotions to inanimate objects.

The spell worked just as well for him as it usually did: All the candles in the room lit up at once. But something began making an unholy racket. Peregrine blinked and peered around the room, growing increasingly confused. The herbs hanging on racks were gone. So were the apothecary jars full of ingredients. The room now stood nearly empty, except for a rocking chair and a crib, neither of which had been used in years.

The crib was the source of the wailing.

Peregrine approached slowly, so as not to startle the crib's occupant, but that small person was already awake and extremely unhappy about the situation. It was a newborn baby whose head was covered by only a few whisps, too young to sit or stand. The baby lay on its back waving its arms and legs as it sobbed.

There was no one else in the room to help, so Peregrine picked up the baby, put it over his shoulder, and patted its back. When that didn't help, he swayed back and forth, singing "The Riddle Song," it being the closest thing to a lullaby he could think of on such short notice. *Soothing a fractious infant* had not been on his plan for the day.

The baby's wailing made Peregrine long to cover his ears, but he did his best to ignore the sound. Instead, he concentrated on his singing. When he grew tired of "The Riddle Song," he switched to "O Waly, Waly." That proved more effective.

Gradually the sobbing turned into hiccupping, and then into blessed silence. He was about to put the baby back in the crib when the door to the nursery creaked open. He turned around to see his older sister, wearing both a warm dressing gown and an ominous glower.

"What are you doing in here?" Abigail hissed at him. "You woke up the baby!"

"Why is there a baby in the nursery?" he whispered back.

"Where else would a baby be?"

Her answer was so rational that it momentarily silenced Peregrine. He put the sleeping baby down in the crib and backed away slowly. Abigail extinguished the lights with a whispered incantation, and both of them sighed with relief when they reached the safety of the hallway and shut the door without waking the baby.

"Whose baby is that?" Peregrine demanded.

Abigail sighed and brushed a strand of loose hair out of her face. "No one knows. I mean, he's a foundling, from the foundling hospital that Keziah Thompson helps manage. Someone left him in the foundling wheel a few weeks ago."

"I see." London probably had no shortage of abandoned infants. "But why is he *here*?" Carrington House was not an orphanage.

"You will have to ask Susan to explain that." Abigail darted a sour look at the nursery door. "This was all *her* idea." She sounded no happier about the matter than Peregrine.

Peregrine knew better than to step in between his sister and her lover when they had a disagreement. That path led to certain doom. So, he changed the subject to something that concerned him personally. "Where did all the *materia magica* go?"

"We put it in Cosmo's room." A yawn interrupted Abigail's explanation. "Most of it, that is. Some of it is in the guest room." Cosmo's old bedchamber had been unused since Valance moved out, back in January, and the guest room had been relegated to storage duty for ages.

"Oh. Very well. But which room is the starflower in?" He'd rather not have to search half the house for a single ingredient.

Abigail threw her hands in the air. "God, Peregrine, I don't know where we put that. Can't you look for it tomorrow?"

"But what if I need it now?" That was, by any estimation, an unlikely scenario, but not impossible.

Abigail glared at him. "If you want to spend all night searching for it, you can. But I am going back to bed. Please don't wake up the baby." She turned on her heel and stalked back to her room.

After she left, it dawned on Peregrine that he did not even know the name of their new housemate. This was all most irregular! He hoped Susan had a good explanation.

CHAPTER SEVEN

ONE AFTERNOON, DORA came downstairs to find the drawing room empty. For once, she had beaten both her sister and brother-in-law in getting dressed for dinner. She sat down on one of the well-padded armchairs and reached for the journal on the nearby tea table. One of the many advantages of living in her sister's house was that she could read the various publications about magic Valance subscribed to.

She'd gotten halfway through an article about using sorcery to magically transport letters across long distances when the butler opened the door. "Mr. Carrington to see you, miss," he announced.

Dora sprang up from her chair. "Peregrine! If you are hoping to be invited to dinner, you are in luck. The cook is making that roasted chicken you like."

She knew she was grinning foolishly at him, but she did not care. It had not even been a full day since she had last seen him, but even that seemed too long. She half hoped he would kiss her, since no one else was in the room, but apparently that possibility did not occur to him.

"I didn't come here for dinner," he explained. "I received an invitation that included you. Or rather, it included Theo Rossini." He handed her a folded piece of expensive paper.

Dora unfolded the note and read it, feeling puzzled until she came to the signature. "Oh, Lord Kellway! I met him at the conference the other day." She hadn't expected him to remember her, though, let alone include her in an invitation to a dinner party. "Do you know him, then?"

Her question seemed to surprise Peregrine. "Of course. He was one of my father's friends. I believe he is Cosmo's godfather, in fact. I wonder if he's disappointed that Cosmo prefers mathematics to magic?"

Dora had no idea how to respond to this speculation, so perhaps it was just as well that Honora's entrance into the dining room prevented her from answering.

"Oh, good afternoon, Mr. Carrington. Are you going to stay for dinner? We are having that chicken that you like."

"If you invite me." Peregrine looked as hopeful as a puppy who smelled bacon in someone's pocket.

"You are always welcome here," Honora said, smiling brightly.

Dora knew that to Peregrine that was no empty courtesy: Peregrine had been a frequent guest at the Valance dinner table even before his betrothal to Dora.

"But it's a good thing I came down before Valance did," Honora added, and her smile fell. "He would say that the two of you ought not be sitting here unchaperoned."

"What nonsense!" Peregrine protested. "It's not as if we are likely to fornicate right here in your drawing room. I mean, there are other surfaces far more comfortable than that *chaise longue*."

Dora darted a quick look at the red plush *chaise longue*. Would it really be uncomfortable? The seat was well padded . . . but what on earth was she *thinking*? Embarrassed by her own thoughts, she flicked her eyes back to her sister and hoped her sudden flush had not visibly pinkened her cheeks.

The corner of Honora's mouth visibly twitched, but she otherwise maintained a serious expression. "I do not believe that would quite assuage Valance's concerns," she said tactfully. "He likes to see the proprieties observed, you know."

"Oh, I know," Dora grumbled. In the short time she'd been in

London, she had already found Valance's propriety chafing.

But she grudgingly accepted that while she lived in Lord Valance's house, she ought to follow his rules. He was the one feeding and clothing her, since she did not have access to her own fortune. That was very generous of him, especially given all the visits to the modiste that Honora insisted on.

Privately, Dora sometimes wished she and Peregrine had stayed in Surrey instead of coming to London for what was left of the Season. No one at Carrington Abbey cared whether or not Dora was chaperoned, though Dora could not have said whether this was because the Carringtons trusted the two of them more than Valance did or because they simply did not care about propriety. (She suspected the latter.)

Moreover, if Dora had stayed in Surrey, she would not have had to worry about avoiding a public scandal, if only because she would not have attended many public events. While she enjoyed London, she would have been perfectly willing to live quietly in the country for a few months if that would convince her guardians of her steadiness and responsibility. The current limbo in which she hung, not knowing when or if her guardians would approve of her marriage, was beginning to strain her nerves.

AT DINNER THAT night, most of the conversation was about the baby that Susan Taylor had brought home from the Foundling Hospital. Both Dora and Honora were surprised that quiet, gentle-tempered Susan had done something so unexpected without discussing it with anyone beforehand.

"It isn't like bringing home a stray dog," Honora pointed out. "Babies require so much attention. Your sister and Miss Taylor will have to hire a nursemaid. Do you think they will take the baby back to the hospital when they see how much work it is?" A worried line formed between her brows.

Dora privately thought Honora's lapdog required as much attention as any two children, but she kept that thought to herself. Honora did not like hearing criticism of Bishop Barkley—no matter how much the dog deserved it.

Valance, however, shook his head. "There's a determined streak in Susan's character. You don't see it very often, but when it comes out, she's implacable. I doubt she will change her mind."

Peregrine nodded. "Susan has put her foot down about this. The baby nearly died of croup, and she took it into her head that the air in the foundling hospital was bad for his lungs. That is why she brought him home."

"But wouldn't the air in Russell Square be just as bad?" Dora protested. It was spring, so there was no need to heat houses, but cookstoves still produced smoke. Between horse droppings in the streets and smoke in the air, even the West End stank—and the odor would only get worse as the weather warmed up.

"Yes, but I maintain enchantments on our house to purify the air," Peregrine explained. "I designed them when Susan moved in, because she is prone to respiratory problems. Her chest colds always last longer than anyone else's."

"Perhaps that is why she felt so strongly about the baby. She knows how awful it is to be overcome by coughing fits." Honora sounded more sympathetic now.

Dora eyed her sister with interest. Lately, Honora seemed increasingly sentimental about children. Did she have a particular reason for that new interest? And if so, when did she plan to announce it?

"She would do better to take the baby to the Abbey," Valance suggested. "If the city air is really what's making him sick, he would fare better in the country."

"Yes, they plan to do that," Peregrine agreed. "But Abigail has some charity event to attend the first week of June, and they hope to stay in town until then." He took the last bite of roast chicken, then looked wistfully down at his empty plate.

Dora knew Peregrine's good manners would prevent him

from taking too much of any one dish on the table, though he clearly liked the roast chicken more than anything else. She took pity on him and placed another serving on his plate.

Peregrine's whole face brightened as he smiled his thanks. When Dora looked away, she caught her sister watching them mistily. Perhaps children were not the only thing Honora had grown sentimental about.

Dora took control of the conversation before her sister could say anything embarrassing. "Do you plan to go to Lord Kellway's dinner party, Peregrine?"

He shrugged. "I suppose I might as well. It probably won't be as bad as most dinner parties. Lord Kellway is a sensible man, and easy to talk to, as long as one can keep him from talking about fossils all the time."

Valance made a choking sound. He had to clear his throat with a sip of wine before speaking. "Isn't that the pot calling the kettle black?"

"I never talk about fossils!" Peregrine protested. "Abigail is the one who went through a fossil phase. *I* never did that."

Honora quickly intervened. "But Dora, he invited *Theo* Rossini. He thinks you are a gentleman. Do you even have a set of men's evening clothes?"

"No. That is a good point." Dora frowned. Honora was right: None of her menswear was formal enough for a dinner party. Why had she not thought of that earlier? There would not be time to have new clothes made, would there? "Perhaps I won't be able to go."

"Oh, I can just explain things to Lord Kellway. You needn't worry."

Everyone stared at Peregrine, who kept happily eating chicken with egg sauce, apparently not noticing the confusion on their faces. (To be fair, though, it was a particularly good recipe.)

Dora raised her eyebrows. "Explain what, exactly? That I was inducted into the Society under false pretenses? That I'm actually a girl? That I am your intended as well as a collaborator on the meteorite spell?"

"Yes, all of that." Peregrine waved away her objections. "Lord Kellway will understand. His granddaughter is a powerful witch, you know. He knows perfectly well that women can be as magically gifted as men."

This seemed to be rather missing the point. Dora was not concerned about how Lord Kellway would view her work as a sorceress. Most people considered magic to be a perfectly respectable hobby for ladies, so long as they did not accept money for their work. Rather, she worried about how he would react to having met her in disguise.

"Don't you think that he might be a bit scandalized at Dora having passed herself off as a young man?" Honora worded the objection more delicately than Dora would have.

"Oh, no! I don't think he will mind that. Why would he?" Peregrine looked from face to face, apparently puzzled by their concern.

Valance shook his head. He held his tongue, but his expression spoke volumes, at least to Dora.

"You can tell him the truth if you want, Peregrine. I don't mind," Dora said. "But I expect Lord Kellway will rescind his invitation when he learns who I really am. Won't that bother you?"

"Yes, that would bother me very much," Peregrine agreed. "But it won't happen. You'll see." He smiled, but she retained all her doubts.

TWO DAYS LATER, an invitation arrived at the Valance house, addressed to *Miss* Rossini. Dora opened it up as soon as she finished breakfast. Wonder of wonders, Peregrine was right: Lord Kellway had invited her to the dinner party under her own name. The invitation included Lord and Lady Valance, too.

"It was kind of him to invite the two of you," Dora observed. So far as she knew, her sister hadn't been on the original guest list.

"It would not have been quite the thing for you to be escorted by Peregrine, since you are not married," Valance explained. "But you can accompany us, since we are your relatives."

Dora sighed, though she suspected he was right. People would judge her if she wandered about town with a young man who was not her husband, father, or brother. "When I am of age," she announced, "I will live the way I want and consign propriety to the Devil, like Abigail Carrington."

She did not fancy writing political essays, as Abigail did. But she would very much enjoy being able to blithely ignore Society. Once she came of age, Uncle Robert and Lady Grantly would have less control over her, though Uncle Robert would still hold the purse strings.

"You need a fortune as big as Abigail's to flaunt social rules that way," Valance warned her. "Unless you have a wealthy godparent who conveniently bequeaths you a fortune before you turn twenty-one, you may be in trouble."

She supposed he had a point. In order to live as unconventionally as the Carringtons did, one probably had to be as rich as they were. Yet another way in which life was unfair.

Dora set the invitation aside and spent the rest of the day trying to think up ways of earning a fortune so she could live independently. Sadly, none of her ideas seemed plausible even to her.

CHAPTER EIGHT

THOUGH HE RARELY looked forward to purely social events, by the evening of Lord Kellway's dinner party, Peregrine was eager for a night away from the nursery. It was good to talk about something other than pap and nappies. He had gotten deep in a conversation with Lukesh Chandra, the secretary of the Cambion Club, when he saw a not-quite stranger—someone he *knew* he'd met, but could not place—bearing down on him.

"Is something wrong?" Mr. Chandra asked. "You look like you've seen a ghost."

"Not a ghost," Peregrine said frantically. "Someone whose name I should know, but don't." He jerked his chin in the direction of the gray-haired man whose forward progress had fortunately been halted by Kellway himself. "Do you know that gentleman?"

Mr. Chandra took a quick look, and his eyebrows shot up. "Mr. Blithfield, you mean?"

"Blithfield! That's the name!" The weight of his panic lifted so quickly, Peregrine felt nearly buoyant. "Right. I met him at the Society of Astronomical Magicians. Do you know him?"

Mr. Chandra's lips tightened. "Yes, but I ought to tell you—" He bit off the end of the sentence when Blithfield popped up in front of them, smiling hopefully. "Good evening, Mr. Blithfield. Charming weather we're having this evening?"

"Isn't it?" Blithfield turned to Peregrine next. "I am so glad to have caught you, Mr. Carrington. I have any number of questions for you."

The club secretary murmured something politely and slipped away before he could be drawn into the conversation. For a moment, Peregrine wondered what Mr. Chandra had been about to tell him, but that was quickly forgotten as he talked with Blithfield about his meteorite enchantment. Peregrine spent a pleasant enough quarter hour explaining the adjustments he hoped would make the spell more accessible.

"The current version of the spell requires both a sorcerer and a wizard to cast, and many magicians do not have partners skilled enough to work it. Or they do not care to work in collaboration," he told Blithfield.

For that matter, Peregrine himself generally preferred to work on his own for most of his spells. Many of his past attempts at collaboration had gone awry because his partners had not wanted to do things Peregrine's way, and he struggled to adapt to their methods. It was most fortunate that he and Dora worked so well together. Unlike many magicians, she understood his thinking well enough to adapt to it.

"Now that I know my original spell works," Peregrine explained, "I hope to modify it so it could be cast by a single wizard."

Once he accomplished that, he wanted to try writing a sorcerous version of the spell: one that did not require a wizard at all. Dora would be extremely helpful with that project; she'd studied magic with a very skilled sorcerer. The challenge would be how to power the spell without *materia magica*. Peregrine knew of no sorcerers strong enough to work such magic on their own. *Maybe* Matthew Holt could pull it off—on a good day, when he was well-rested and well-fed—but so far as Peregrine knew, Holt had no interest in astronomy. Holt was more of a theoretician than an experimental magician, anyway.

By the time Peregrine got halfway through this explanation, Mr. Blithfield's eyes looked glassy. It dawned on Peregrine that

Blithfield might have no idea who Matthew Holt or Sir Isaac Grantly were. Peregrine knew nothing about Blithfield's own magical background. He'd spent so much time talking about his own pet project that he had not given Blithfield a chance to say anything about his work.

He hastened to rectify his discourtesy. "If you don't mind my asking, are you a wizard or a sorcerer?"

"Neither," Blithfield replied. "I am a mage, but not a particularly powerful one. I have a little talent here, a little talent there—a touch of healing, a touch of empathy, that sort of thing. My interest in magic is largely theoretical." He smiled cheerfully. "But I am very fascinated by your work, even though it is not a spell that I could ever cast myself."

He leaned forward, then, and whispered, as if about to reveal a secret. "The fact of the matter is, Mr. Carrington, that I am part of a consortium of magicians in the North of England. Not a large society, mind you, just a gathering of local magicians from Cumberland, Westmorland, and Northumberland. We are having our annual gathering at the end of this month, and I wondered if you would be interested—"

Before he could finish his sentence, the butler opened the drawing-room door to announce dinner. Peregrine had hoped to snag a seat next to Dora, but Lady Kellway kept a firm hand on the seating arrangements. She directed Peregrine to sit next to her granddaughter, Lady Markham.

Peregrine did not mind, though. Lady Markham moved in the same magical circles the Carringtons did. She had played with Peregrine when they were children and danced with him when they were young adults. She was the strongest magician in the Kellway family, after her grandfather, and she did not object to discussing magic at the dinner table, though the topic was supposedly not polite in mixed company.

Lady Valance took the chair at Peregrine's other hand, which was also a relief. He hadn't known Honora as long as he'd known Lady Markham, but she was the wife of one of his oldest friends, not to mention the sister of his intended bride. By now, he could talk to her about almost anything.

Though the dinner party passed much less awkwardly than usual, Peregrine did not get a chance to approach Dora until the gentlemen rejoined the ladies in the drawing room after dinner. By then, he had used up all his capacity for conversation. He sank into a chair, smiled at Dora, and watched idly as she chattered about gardening with Lady Markham.

It was pleasant to be near Dora at last, but he could not help thinking that he would have been much more comfortable sitting by the fire at home, in his own familiar armchair, either reading a book or listening to Susan recite her newest poems.

The food would have been better at home, too. Peregrine did not care for fancy French cuisine, but the cook at Carrington House knew perfectly well what he liked and what he did not like. She always made at least one thing he could eat. He preferred his own port to the vintage Lord Kellway served, too.

The one drawback to Carrington House was that Dora did not live there. Not yet. And who knew when he would have her? Her uncle did not seem disposed to condone the marriage, even though Valance held the mortgage on the Grantly estate. Even though the son of a baronet ought to have been a perfectly acceptable suitor for Sir Isaac Grantly's daughter. Peregrine could not think of a single good reason for Robert Grantly to reject his suit. Was it pure stubbornness?

Peregrine sometimes entertained the thought of marrying without the permission of Dora's guardian and letting the chips fall where they might. But he had promised Roderick that he wouldn't elope to Scotland, and the more socially acceptable options presented difficulties. If they called the banns in Dora's home parish, the Grantlys would contest them on the grounds that Dora did not have parental consent to marry.

Dora had only just turned nineteen, and the two years before she would come of age seemed like an eternity. How many evenings like this must they spend, clutching at whatever scraps of time together they could grasp?

"Peregrine?" Dora prompted.

He stopped woolgathering and took a real look at his love. Her thick, dark eyelashes accentuated the wideness of her blue-green eyes. If they'd been alone, he would have taken her face in his hands and kissed her thoroughly. But he could not do that here.

"You look lost in thought. What are you thinking of?"

"About how much I want to kiss you." He spoke softly, so no one else would hear, but Dora's eyes widened, and a faint blush rose on her cheeks. Probably that was the sort of thing a gentleman was not supposed to say to a young lady, even if he intended to marry her. "Well, you asked!" he reminded her.

She grinned her mischievous grin. "I did ask. And I love that you always answer my questions honestly." She leaned closer and planted a light kiss on his cheek. Then she turned away to talk to someone else, leaving him sitting in surprised and happy silence. Perhaps there were advantages to dining out now and then, after all.

But on his way out, Peregrine's happiness was shattered when someone tugged his coat sleeve. He yanked his arm free and whirled around to see who'd had the bad manners to touch him unexpectedly. He supposed he should not have been surprised to see a now-familiar round face and steel-gray hair.

"Ah, Mr. Blithfield. Was there something you wanted?" An evening spent in company had left Peregrine feeling like the burnt-out stub of a candle, and his voice sounded sharper and shorter than he'd intended.

"I am so sorry to startle you, Mr. Carrington. It was just that I never got to explain about the house party I plan to host at the end of the month."

Peregrine frowned. "House party? Why should you explain about that?" Blithfield was not one of Peregrine's few close friends. He was merely a colleague with whom Peregrine had had a few minutes of conversation. (Well, maybe more than a few.)

There could be no reason for him to tell Peregrine about his social plans for the summer.

Blithfield made a wry grimace. "I am explaining this badly. The fact of the matter is that our local society of magicians—the Cumberland Thaumaturgical Society—typically meet at someone's house for a week at the beginning of June. Our gathering is one part scholarly meeting, one part gentlemen's house party. We drink and chat and ramble about the country, that sort of thing." He smiled hopefully.

"Cumberland Thaumaturgical Society," Peregrine mused. "Didn't Ned Anderson go to one of those gatherings last year?" Or maybe not; that had been about the time that Ned fell ill.

The other man blinked. "Mr. Anderson, the sorcerer? Yes, he might have been there. I don't quite recall." He shrugged apologetically. "But it's certainly the case that other members of the Cambion Club have joined us during past summer gatherings."

"You don't say." Peregrine thought he saw where this was going, and he did not like it. He took a step backward, though physical distance often failed to protect him from unwanted invitations.

But his attempted retreat did not deter Mr. Blithfield. "I am certain that my colleagues would love to hear about your meteorite spell. Would you consider doing me the honor of being my house guest?" Blithfield's hopeful smile widened, as if he thought displaying more of his teeth would make the invitation more appealing. Peregrine could think of few things less appealing than traveling all the way to Cumberland to stay at the house of a virtual stranger. He had so many objections he did not know where to start.

"I am afraid I do not attend house parties," Peregrine said gently. "I have rather delicate nerves." He knew perfectly well that "delicate nerves" sounded like the kind of condition that plagued wealthy women with too much time on their hands, but he couldn't think of a better way to explain himself. "I must be a homebody at heart; traveling unsettles me." He twisted his mouth into a rueful smile, hoping to remove any offense from his rejection.

He did not mind going back and forth between Carrington Abbey and the London townhouse. That journey was short, and in either location, he could be certain of a comfortable bed, a good meal, and familiar surroundings. But he'd never liked traveling for seaside holidays, house parties, or visiting relatives. Even if he could be sure of finding comfortable quarters on arrival, being away from home left him out of sorts. For a very dear friend or relation, he might make such a journey. But not for a stranger.

"I will have to decline your very generous offer." He did his best to decline the invitation gracefully, but Blithfield's face still fell.

"Perhaps another year?" Blithfield suggested.

"Perhaps," Peregrine granted. But he privately thought Blithfield would have to wait until the coming of the Coquecigrues before Peregrine came to his house party.

CHAPTER NINE

Dora, who had expected any social event hosted by Lord Kellway to be frightfully awkward, actually had a perfectly lovely evening. When Lord Kellway greeted his guests before dinner, he smiled and said that it was good to see her again. He said nothing about the disguise she had worn when they first met. Only the hint of amusement in his voice indicated that he remembered the circumstances in which they had first met.

But when the guests began to leave after dinner, Lord Kellway approached. "You must be a very good actress, Miss Rossini, because you certainly fooled me at last week's meeting." A faint smile tugging at the corners of his mouth transformed the austere set of his lips.

Dora flushed. "I am sorry for introducing myself under false pretenses—"

He cut her off with a shake of his head. "I know no other way in which you could have attended the meeting, since women are not allowed as members, and the Society tends not to welcome guests. Even I had trouble securing an invitation, and I am well known in magical circles."

That was an understatement if ever she'd heard one! As the president of the Cambion Club and a board member of the Royal Academy of Wizardry, Lord Kellway wielded enormous influence.

"I hope," he continued, "you found the conference interesting."

"Oh, it was fascinating!" At least, the part where two aging magicians nearly came to fisticuffs. Maybe not so much the later papers. "Did you make any discoveries about the, er, ungentlemanly behavior?"

Lord Kellway's eyes widened. Maybe he'd forgotten that he ever mentioned that matter to Dora. "Unfortunately not." His eyes shifted as he glanced at something across the room.

Dora turned her eyes the same way. Lord Kellway seemed to be looking at a group of middle-aged ladies and gentlemen who stood chatting and laughing near the doorway. Dora saw nothing in the least bit suspicious about any of them, but the corners of Lord Kellway's mouth turned down as he watched the group. Interesting.

When Lord Kellway turned back to Dora, his face relaxed. "I hope you enjoy what is left of the Season, Miss Rossini."

"Oh, I am sure I will." Dora recognized a dismissal when she heard one. "Thank you very much for inviting me, sir."

She found Honora and Valance, who were also ready to leave. As they headed into the hall, she glanced back over her shoulder at the mysterious group of people who'd drawn Lord Kellway's disapproval.

Then an idea struck her. "Honora," she whispered to her sister, "are any of those people magicians?" She jerked her chin in their direction, hoping no one else would notice.

Honora narrowed her eyes as she surveyed the group. "There's a mage and a sorceress," she murmured back. "Neither one looks very powerful."

Unlike Dora, Honora could not work any kind of magic. But she could do something Dora could not: She could tell at a glance whether a person had a magical talent, and if so, what sort. Most magicians had some ability to detect magic in use, or sense the traces of past spells, but that was very different from recognizing that another person had magical abilities. Reading auras was a form of magecraft, far less common than sorcery or wizardry.

"Why do you ask?" Honora searched Dora's face.

She smiled her brightest smile in return. "Oh, no reason. Just trying to sort out who's who in Society."

Dora saw no reason to share her extremely vague suspicions. For all she knew, Lord Kellway might be investigating nothing worse than someone refusing to pay a debt of honor. Though why the president of the Cambion Club would care about something like that remained unclear, given that the club did not allow gambling. But really, how much trouble could someone get into at a gentlemen's club?

She kept thinking about the matter as she settled into the Valance family carriage. Dora's elders would undoubtedly have told her that Lord Kellway's investigations were none of her business, that she ought not waste her time wondering about the matter. But Dora believed knowledge was power. In a world where even wealthy women lacked control over their own lives, and illegitimate daughters of country gentlemen were at a distinct disadvantage, even if they possessed magical gifts, she hoarded every scrap of knowledge she found.

One never knew when information would prove unexpectedly useful, or when new social connections might prove advantageous. For example, Dora's life-long friendship with Tom Robson had allowed her to learn details about the slang that schoolboys used, the way they walked, and the way they acted in public. That information had proven very useful when she needed to disguise herself. Nearly as useful as the clothes Tom loaned her, in fact.

Dora was well aware that being in Lord Kellway's good graces could be a social advantage. Dora's father had been a sorcerer; her brother-in-law was a sorcerer; her betrothed was a wizard. Those connections firmly placed her in the orbit of the Cambion Club, even though women could not be members of that august body. Any connections she made in the magical community might be useful to either her or her extended family in the future.

"Dora," Lord Valance said, "what are you thinking about?

You look so serious."

"Oh, I was just thinking about ways to expand my social credit."

"Is that so?"

Valance had illuminated the carriage with one of his light spells, so Dora could see the confusion written all over her brother-in-law's face. She chuckled, then took pity on him. "I was thinking about ways to build connections that might benefit Peregrine's research."

"He does well enough working with the magical community," Valance told her. "It's the general public that sometimes poses a challenge. He gets bored by social events where none of the guests share his interests."

Privately, Dora thought that anyone could be bored by such events. But she kept that thought to herself. "Speaking of social events, have we many engagements this week?" she asked instead.

"Only a couple," Honora told her. "I am afraid that Valance and I are homebodies. But if there are any invitations you particularly wish us to accept, you have only to ask."

"I would like to go to a masquerade at the Argyll Rooms." Dora put on her best plaintive, wistful young lady voice. She did want to go, but she wanted to rattle her brother-in-law even more.

His response met all of her expectations. "Proper young ladies do not go to Argyll Room balls!" He looked positively horrified. "That is the sort of place gentlemen go with their—in disreputable company."

"Oh, did you ever go there with your mistress?" Honora sounded genuinely curious rather than judgmental, but Valance turned an interesting color. He stared out the window rather than looking either of the sisters in the face. "I have not been there in years, and it is not an appropriate place for Dora to visit." He scowled and left it at that.

Dora smiled to herself. When her eyes chanced to meet her

sister's, a reciprocal smile flickered across Honora's face. Apparently, Dora was not the only one occasionally amused by Valance's stodginess. Her own smile deepened. It felt so good to be with Honora again. She had missed this during the months they were apart.

She only hoped her guardians accepted their defeat and did not try to separate the sisters again.

A FEW DAYS after the dinner party at Kellway House, Peregrine showed up at the Valance house with a letter in hand and a look of confusion on his face. "I don't know why this Mr. Blithfield is so persistent about asking me to visit him," he grumbled. "I thought I made it clear I had no interest in traveling to Cumberland for this magical house party."

"Magical house party?" For a moment, Dora's imagination filled with the most unlikely visions: a ballroom lit entirely in witchlights, musical instruments that played themselves (was such a thing even possible?), and guests glamoured to look like mythical creatures.

"The house party is also a gathering of magicians from the north of England," Peregrine clarified. "All of the guests are members of the same organization."

Dora sighed, recognizing that her fantasy was just that. As usual, reality was far more mundane. But if she were ever outrageously rich, that would be the sort of party she'd host. She would have to hire a culinary wizard to make the refreshments, and perhaps a green witch to arrange the flowers—or would such an entertainment need something more unique than flowers?

The conversation brought her back to earth before she could wander too far in her flight of fancy.

"If you lived in the north of England, it might be a very useful organization," Valance was saying to Peregrine. "But under the circumstances, it's hard to see what a group of magicians in Cumberland has to do with you."

"Precisely," Peregrine agreed. "I see no reason to travel for days to a house party that I wouldn't enjoy anyway."

"Strange that this Mr. Blithfield is pursuing you so tenaciously, though." Dora picked up the letter of invitation and read it again. Mr. Blithfield practically begged Peregrine to come to his home so he could talk about his meteorite spell. "If he really wants to know more about your work, he can just wait for the proceedings of this year's meeting to be published."

Unless what Blithfield really wanted was the cachet of hosting the magical lion of the Season? It sounded as if he wanted Peregrine's company, not just his research. Alas for Mr. Blithfield, Peregrine did not care for the company of strangers.

"Yes, I thought I made my refusal clear enough at the Kellways' dinner party." Peregrine wrinkled his nose.

"Oh, he was there? I must have been introduced to him, but I don't recall it." Try as she might, she could not summon a face to match the name.

"He is not particularly memorable," Peregrine explained. "And there is no reason why you should remember a middle-aged mage from Cumberland." He folded the letter up and tucked it into his waistcoat pocket. "You need not worry about him. You will probably never see him again."

CHAPTER TEN

D INING WITH THE Valances was, in Peregrine's opinion, about a hundred times more comfortable than attending a formal dinner party. Knowing that he was a picky eater, Honora always made sure their cook prepared something he liked. And after dinner, no one minded if he and Dora sat in a corner and talked only to each other. He would rather have had Dora living with him, but he supposed this was better than the situation of many courting couples, who might only see each other at dinner parties and balls.

"We ought to have you to dine at Carrington House," Peregrine told Valance before he left. "But with Susan's baby in the house, everything is at sixes and sevens." His sister might not want to play hostess when her hands were so full.

"You shouldn't call him *Susan's* baby!" Valance shook his head. "If someone overhears you, they will think she had a child out of wedlock. You might accidentally start some very unpleasant rumors." Valance possessed a rather daunting scowl that transformed his whole expression, and he employed it now.

Peregrine was very familiar with that look of disapproval, but it made no sense here. "No one who knows us would think that! And it *is* her baby. She has no intention of ever taking him back to the foundling hospital. She and Abby are already talking about what school they should send him to in a decade or so."

Peregrine had been a little surprised to learn that young Samuel Hodges (such being the foundling's name) was to remain at Carrington House indefinitely. But the London townhouse had been left jointly to all five of the Carrington children, so Abigail had a perfect right to keep whatever housemates she wanted. He had simply never imagined she would add such a loud, needy occupant to the household without any warning.

When he returned to Russell Square that night, he was forcibly reminded that his home was not the quiet refuge it had been in the past. The little gentleman in the nursery was having a bad night again. Though the nursery was on the third floor, Peregrine could hear him once he reached the top of the first flight of stairs. He kept climbing, guessing his help might be needed.

He found Susan holding a screaming, red-faced baby and a feeding cup full of pap. Or rather, the cup *had* been full of pap, but most of it now covered Susan's dressing gown. Peregrine took young Mr. Hodges so Susan could wipe herself off.

"Where is Simmons?" he asked. The nurse who'd been hired to look after the baby would probably have the best chance of calming him down.

Susan wrinkled her nose. "I gave her the night off because it's her mother's birthday. Her mother is turning sixty."

Peregrine snorted. Simmons's mother's age was immaterial. What mattered was that Simmons, who had years of experience caring for young children, was out. They were on their own.

"I thought Sam was hungry," Susan explained, "but he wouldn't drink. He kept pushing the cup away until it spilled."

"I see that." Peregrine studied Susan for a moment. There were bags under her eyes, and exhaustion pinched her face "How long have you been at this?"

She shrugged. "It felt like hours, but it probably wasn't that long."

"Go to bed. I will get him back to sleep." When she opened her mouth to argue, he forestalled her. "I have more experience with babies than you do." Roderick had two daughters, and Peregrine had been home during the Long Vacation when Lilias was a newborn. He'd been frequently put to work entertaining his niece or soothing her to sleep.

"If you insist," Susan reluctantly conceded. She dabbed ineffectively at the mess on her dressing gown. "If you need a break, wake Abby up. It's *her* turn next."

When the door closed behind her, Peregrine sat down in the rocking chair and addressed Samuel directly. "It takes an entire house of adults to look after you, young man. How in the world did you survive in the foundling hospital?"

He decided, after thinking about it for a moment, that he would rather not know what Samuel's life had been like before coming to Carrington House. Orphanages and foundling institutions were typically understaffed, weren't they? There would not have been a trio of young adults who had the time to constantly hold a baby, or rock him, or sooth him. Samuel's caregivers would probably have laid him down in a crib and left him to cry.

"I suppose Susan might have known what she was doing when she brought you here," Peregrine conceded. The house might be more crowded now, but there was no shortage of people on hand to comfort the baby when he was inconsolable.

Samuel did not seem to be soothed by this reminder of his improved living conditions. Nor did rocking comfort him tonight. He only fell asleep when Peregrine began walking around the room, singing all the lullabies he could remember. As soon as Peregrine tried to put the baby down in his crib, he woke up and screamed again. They ended up pacing back and forth in the nursery for what seemed like hours, until Abigail came in for the next feeding.

"This baby is going to be the death of us all," Peregrine predicted. Neither Lilias nor Juliana had been anything like this fussy when they were newborns! "Might he be unwell? Ought we consult a physician? Or an apothecary? Maybe there's a potion that can soothe a crying child."

"Potions like that are usually full of laudanum, or something equally harmful." Abigail took Samuel from Peregrine's arms, shifting him as gingerly as possible, but neither of them was surprised that Samuel woke up anyway.

"Nostrums for children are full of quackery," Abigail continued. "I would only trust a reliable physician to diagnose him. But I think he's just colicky, anyway. Simmons says that colic peaks at about two months. Things should start improving soon. Of course," she added more doubtfully, "babies don't always do what they are supposed to do."

Peregrine and Abigail both studied the baby. Samuel must have been hungry this time, because he stopped fussing in order to guzzle the contents of the feeding cup. That was a promising sign, wasn't it? In Peregrine's (admittedly limited) experience, babies usually grew sleepy once their bellies were full.

"I hope you are right about the colic ending soon," Peregrine said. "Our nerves are all going to be shattered if this keeps up." He hurried to his own room before Samuel could start crying again.

HAVING STAYED UP so late into the night with the baby, Peregrine slept later into the morning than was his wont. He slept so late, in fact, that he woke up with a headache. His plans for the day all had to be adjusted, because he could not focus well enough to work magic.

He spent the morning answering letters instead. That required less concentration.

When he got to Mr. Blithfield's invitation to the house party, he hesitated. Most of his reasons for declining the invitation still stood. But now, after such a rough night, it occurred to him that getting out of the house for a couple of weeks might have benefits. Surely Samuel would be over the worst of his colic by the time Peregrine returned.

On the one hand, it did not seem quite fair to leave Abigail and Susan to care for the baby themselves. On the other hand, no one had consulted Peregrine before adding a baby to the household, though he had as much ownership in the townhome as his sister did. How would they like it if *he* brought some stranger home to live with them?

Instead of writing a firm refusal, Peregrine set Mr. Blithfield's letter aside and walked to his club—only to find a crowd gathered outside the building and smoke billowing up from it.

The Cambion Club in flames? *Inconceivable!* Somehow, the solid ground of Peregrine's everyday life had become quicksand. Was nothing safe anymore?

Peregrine caught sight of the club secretary, and hurried towards him. If anyone knew what had happened, Mr. Chandra would.

"What happened?" Peregrine had to shout to be heard over the murmuring crowd.

Mr. Chandra shook his head. "A fire broke out in the smoking room," he explained. "It seems someone emptied the ashes from their pipe into a wastepaper basket. It caught fire, and since there was no one left in the room, it went up in flames. The fire spread to the dining room."

"Well, damn." The words hardly seemed adequate to this catastrophe, but Peregrine could think of nothing better to say. The smoking room seemed no loss to him (smoking being a filthy habit), but the dining room was the heart of the club. There were members who joined purely for the quality of the table and cellars.

Mr. Chandra studied Peregrine for a moment. "I can see that you are worried," he said kindly. "Don't fret too much. There are a couple of sorcerers working to bring the fire under control magically. They are making good progress. I do not believe it will spread further." His face fell. "But I imagine it'll take weeks or months to repair the damage."

Peregrine felt a strange sinking in the vicinity of his digestive organs. "Do you suppose the club will be closed while it is being repaired?"

"Yes, of course. It will be closed for a few weeks at the very least."

"Wait, does that mean you are homeless for now?" Didn't Mr. Chandra live at the club? If so, he had far more reason to panic than Peregrine did.

But the secretary shook his head. "No, I took chambers elsewhere when I married. But there were a few members in residence who will have to find temporary lodging."

"And all of us will have to find a new reading room," Peregrine grumbled.

Mr. Chandra slanted a considering glance at him. "You are not a member anywhere else?"

"No." Some members, like Valance, did maintain memberships at other clubs. But Peregrine had seen no reason to put his name in for White's or Boodle's when he came down from Oxford. Carringtons always belonged to the Cambion Club! No other club in London sustained anything like the vibrant intellectual life of its common rooms.

Peregrine had relied on the club ever since he moved to London. Since many of its members were practicing magicians, the Cambion Club was the place to go when one needed to consult another magician. Since the club employed one of the best chefs in all the London clubs, it was also the source of a reliably good meal. Perhaps most importantly, the club was Peregrine's escape when he quarreled with his sister and needed a quiet room where he could hide behind a book and not be bothered. Conversation was not even *allowed* in the reading room.

Peregrine gazed mournfully at the smoking building. Between the loss of the club and the colicky baby at home, his entire life seemed to have been completely overturned. He did not like that one bit.

Maybe he should go down to Carrington Abbey early this year. There were no babies or house fires there. He thought, once again, of Mr. Blithfield's letter. Perhaps he ought to consider accepting that invitation after all. A house party still seemed terrible, but it could not be worse than *this*.

Another rough night with Samuel convinced him. The next day, he wrote back to Mr. Blithflield, explaining that he found it in his power to accept Blithfield's kind invitation after all. After the house party, he would head to Surrey for the family gathering his mother wanted. By that point, little Samuel Hodges would supposedly be out of the fussiest stage of infancy, so there ought to be less crying at home. If Peregrine was very lucky, the club might be open again, too. One could hope!

CHAPTER ELEVEN

"YOU ARE TAKING Mr. Carrington's absence very well," Honora told Dora at breakfast one morning. "I was afraid you would mope with him gone."

Dora restrained the urge to roll her eyes. "I don't mope," she reminded her sister. "Moping accomplishes nothing." Better to conserve one's energies for a more practical use—trying to outwit her guardians, for example. Uncle Robert's most recent letter had suggested that Dora compromise by waiting a year before marrying. She was less than thrilled by this suggestion.

Her lack of moping didn't mean that she didn't mind Peregrine's absence. She missed him very much. It had been very disappointing to learn that she would have to go from seeing him nearly every day to being apart from him for weeks.

She was also annoyed that she could not accompany him. She had helped him with both the calculations for his meteorite spell and with casting the enchantment itself. He'd written the bulk of the spell, true, but she'd made some significant contributions. In a perfect world, she would have accompanied him to any presentations, conferences, or meetings at which he discussed their work.

But they did not live in a perfect world, and an unmarried woman who traveled in company with an unrelated bachelor would be assumed to be no better than she ought to be. She could not afford such a scandal now, when she was still trying to convince Uncle Robert of her good sense and maturity.

So, Dora stayed behind when Peregrine set off for Cumberland. Though she did not mope or repine, she *did* silently grumble to herself. She'd thought that becoming engaged would bring her closer to her lover, but instead, their interactions seemed to be increasingly restricted by rules that both she and Peregrine thought foolish and unnecessary.

Though she did not like to admit it even to herself, there were times she resented Peregrine for leaving London. Why must he keep attending events at which she was not welcome? Wouldn't it have been grand if he'd refused to attend the house party without his partner, purely as a matter of principle? That idea never seemed to have occurred to Peregrine.

But nursing her discontent would help no one, so Dora sought better uses of her time. She decided to ask her brother-in-law to teach her his method of casting spells. Before she met Valance, she had never heard of a sorcerer who worked magic through written signs. She wanted to see how it worked.

Unfortunately, his method of casting spells did not work for Dora. Writing *lux* on a piece of paper did nothing, though speaking the word and snapping her fingers summoned a violet-colored witchlight.

"You have to pour magic into the pen strokes," Valance explained. "Without magic, it's just ink on paper."

But try as she might, Dora could not figure out how to do that. She knew how to work magic with spoken words, but she did not understand what it meant to "pour magic into the pen strokes."

She finally gave up and put her pen down. "I don't see how you do this at all!" Respect and frustration mingled in her voice.

Valance shrugged. "I don't see how you work magic by speaking. Everyone's magic works differently."

"Fair enough." Usually not *this* differently, though.

Dora decided to give it one last shot. This time, as she carefully printed the word *lux*, she spoke it aloud, too. The ball of light that burst into being above the table shone so brightly, she automatically covered her eyes.

"Now that's very interesting." Valance shaded his eyes with one hand while he peered up at the witchlight. "Combining written and spoken words seems to have amplified the spell, making the light brighter. I wonder if other sorcerers could do that? It might be very useful. We ought to test this out with some of the fellows at the club... Not that you would be allowed across the threshold." He sighed.

"The Cambion Club is closed for repairs, anyway," Dora reminded him. But she thought Valance brought up a good point. It really wasn't fair that so many of the important conversations in the magical world took place in exclusively male spaces.

"When Peregrine gets back," Valance suggested, "we could have a dinner party and invite a couple of sorcerers to talk it over."

Dora nodded. Perhaps there were other ways around the restrictions. "Abigail knows many of the lady magicians in town," she pointed out. "Some of them are sorceresses. I might be able to work with them." If gentleman magicians could have exclusive clubs, why not lady magicians?

After that success, Dora spent nearly an hour exploring simple sorceries to see what other spoken spells might be augmented with writing. The amplification technique did not seem to work with all spells, and she could not understand why. Valance suggested trying spells that were already intrinsically affiliated with the written word, such as the one she'd recently learned for sending a letter from one location to another.

That was such a happy thought that she wanted to investigate it immediately. She wrote a short note to her brother and sealed it with wax. But instead of writing the address on the outside of the paper, she wrote out the text of the sending spell, directing it to Jack's bedroom on the first story of Grantly Manor. She could not be certain that his mother would give him a letter from her if it were sent through the usual mail, but if the spell worked, Dora could circumvent Lady Grantly entirely.

When she spoke the last word, the letter disappeared. The vacuum left by its passing created a tiny breeze that ruffled the loose papers littering the worktable.

Dora blinked. "That was much easier than usual."

Transporting something miles away took a great deal of magical energy, and though Dora was a skilled magician, she was only moderately powerful. Normally, working a spell like this would have drawn enough of her power to make her feel the loss, like a muscle sore from overuse. Today, she felt nothing . . . until her stomach growled.

"I think we ought to ask the cook to send up some luncheon for us," Valance suggested tactfully. "Dinner is still a long time away."

Dora agreed, and they ceased their experiments for the day.

SHE SPENT THE rest of that week playing with the new technique. The letter spell was particularly useful while Peregrine was away. Instead of waiting for the royal mail to carry Dora's letters, she could send them to him nearly instantly—though she was then left waiting for his reply. Peregrine had many virtues, but answering correspondence quickly was not one of them.

Peregrine had, in fact, intended to let all his mail pile up in the library at Carrington House during his absence. When his sister expressed some concern about the wisdom of this plan, he shrugged his shoulders and suggested that Dora could answer all the correspondence related to his magic.

"But you don't want me reading through your mail, do you?" Dora had protested. They might be betrothed, but allowing her access to his private correspondence still required enormous trust.

"Why not?" He smiled at her. "It is not as if I have any dark secrets. The worst you could find out is how much I spend at the bookseller each month."

"I should think that was shocking enough," Abigail said dryly.

They all laughed, but Peregrine had been serious about allowing Dora to read his mail. Before he left for Cumberland, he arranged to have it delivered to Dora every day during his absence. She was supposed to respond to letters about their work if she could, and forward anything that needed Peregrine's immediate attention. The additional practice with the letter-sending spell was pretty much the only silver lining to Peregrine's absence.

Most of Peregrine's correspondence was excessively boring. Even the bill from the bookstore was less shocking than she'd expected. But a few days after Peregrine safely reached Corbin Hall, a letter arrived that shook Dora's composure.

The letter must have been somehow mislaid—though it had been posted in London, it was dated more than a week ago. It was from Lord Kellway, so Dora assumed that it had something to do with Peregrine's magical work.

But the letter had quite a different subject.

My dear Mr. Carrington,

I hope you will not take this letter amiss. Consider it merely a word of warning from one of your father's old friends. The fact of the matter is that I am concerned I may have inadvertently put you in the way of an extremely undesirable acquaintanceship.

At last week's dinner party, I saw you in conversation with Mr. Blithfield. I regret to inform you that Mr. Blithfield was there not in the capacity of a friend or a colleague, but as the subject of an investigation. To put it bluntly, I have heard the most alarming rumors about him. Naturally, I can say nothing about the content of these rumors, other than that I worry he may be trying to gain your confidence for purposes which could do you no good.

Speaking in both my professional capacity as a magician and as an old family friend, I recommend you avoid contact with Blithfield as much as possible. By no means should you allow him into your confidence on the subject of your research. He may not be worthy of your trust. Under no circumstances should you share magical formulas or written spells with him, unless they have already been published.

I apologize for not having spoken to you earlier. The conflagration at the Cambion Club has occupied most of my attention, as I am sure you can imagine. If you have any questions, you are free to call on me.

Until we meet again, I remain your servant,
Kellway

Dora read the letter three times to make certain she understood it. But there could be no misinterpreting Lord Kellway's plain speaking. Mr. Blithfield posed some sort of threat to her intended bridegroom. And her intended was, at this moment, a guest at Blithfield's house, and entirely at his mercy.

Clearly, she would have to do something about it.

CHAPTER TWELVE

June, 1817

PEREGRINE REGRETTED COMING to Corbin Hall nearly as soon as he got there. The journey had been long and tiring, and he arrived just in time to dress for dinner. That meant no time to recover from traveling. The last post chaise he'd rented had been horribly sprung, and the postilions urged the horses along far too quickly, despite the poor state of the country roads. All the jolting left him aching to the bone.

Dinner that first night revealed that the company gathered at the house party might be devoted to magic, but they were also partial to drinking too much after dinner and talking loudly long into the night. It was every bit as dreadful as his worst fears. He pled exhaustion and retired while the rest of the gentlemen were still chattering loudly.

A footman had been assigned to serve as his valet, but Peregrine saw no need to call him. He was used to dressing and undressing himself; he did not particularly like being touched by strangers. He would not have minded Dora undressing him, he thought wistfully. Not that there was any chance of that happening any time soon, given Robert Grantly's stubborn refusal to condone the marriage.

When he got into bed, he discovered that the mattress was lumpy. Corbin Hall was a stately-looking manor, but somehow it did not seem quite as comfortable as other country houses he'd visited. He doubted he would sleep well, despite his fatigue.

As he shifted around in bed, trying to find a more comfortable position, Peregrine wondered if he ought to write to Abigail for help. His sister knew perfectly well how little he enjoyed this sort of visit, and she had promised that if he needed an excuse to leave early, she would invent an emergency: a family member with a broken leg, a distant uncle on his deathbed, whatever it might take. He disliked lying, even so-called white lies, but the idea tempted him.

But perhaps, he told himself, he would adjust to the new setting, and the other guests would prove more tolerable as he got to know them better. At the worst, he would only be here for two weeks. Anyone could survive that . . . or at least, a sufficiently high percentage of people to justify the word *anyone*.

He wished he could have brought Dora with him, though. He already missed her, and she might have helped him ease his way into conversations. He could talk about his work readily enough, but discussions involving other subjects exhausted him. Dora was much better at a light chat than he was, and he could have sat back and let her do the talking. That would have relieved much of the stress of his visit.

But Dora had not been invited. Peregrine was on his own.

OVER THE NEXT few days, Peregrine grew accustomed to the rhythm of the house party. After breakfast each morning, the guests would gather in the formal drawing room. The large room had been furnished in the latest mode, but it currently resembled a lecture hall or classroom rather than a parlor. Rows of padded mahogany armchairs were set up at one end of the room each morning, then moved back into place each evening, so the room could be used for its more traditional social functions.

The rows of chairs faced a plain wooden table of golden oak. The table had clearly been brought in from another room, because it did not match any of the other furniture. But, being counter height, it was perfect for working magic. The heavy wooden podium next to the table was made of some darker wood that did not match the table, and that contrast irritated Peregrine to no end. Would it have been so very hard to have found furniture that matched?

Each morning, one or two magicians would share either a paper about their work or a practical demonstration of a new spell, after which the whole group spent some time discussing these presentations. Later, conversations about magic often began again at dinner and continued into the evening.

But the afternoon hours were exclusively given up to recreation, and they posed Peregrine's biggest challenge. It was not the season for hunting, but Corbin Hall lay so near to the bank of the river Eden that guests could easily wander over to fish for salmon or trout, weather allowing. Most of the guests seemed to enjoy this very much, but Peregrine did not. He liked having fresh-caught fish at dinner, but he had never learned to angle and he did not care to learn now. He was perfectly content to let other people catch his dinner.

The first day, he accompanied the anglers out of curiosity. For a time, he strolled along the bank, watching while his companions fished. When the novelty of fishing wore off, Peregrine excused himself and wandered off to explore the grounds. He stumbled across a gravel path that paralleled the river. Heavy tree cover shaded the path, allowing him to walk in comfort despite the warm day.

When he found a comfortable bench, Peregrine sat down and sketched the wildflowers that lined the path. Next time he wrote to Dora, he would tuck that picture into the letter. A picture would not smell as sweet as a real violet, but it would travel better. That way Dora could get a glimpse of what he saw, though she could not be here to accompany him.

The woods were pleasant, and Peregrine would not have minded coming here each day, if not for the risk of running into other house guests. He was not, after all, the only man who enjoyed a walk in the shade on a hot summer day. Peregrine simply could not spend an entire day in other people's company. He needed time and space to himself in order to recover from the morning's activities. Otherwise, he would not be able to face the daily dinner table conversations.

After that first day, he left the anglers alone and avoided the river except when he thought it likely to be deserted. Instead of recreating outside, he typically retired to the library to read. The library, at least, was everything he could have asked for. Mr. Blithfield came from a long line of magicians who had spent centuries adding both theoretical and practical books of magic to the collection.

Most of the books had to do with magecraft or sorcery—those being the types of magic most common among the Blithfields of the past—but the library contained a surprising number of books of wizardry, too. There were a few rare books that had never yet crossed Peregrine's path. If nothing else, this visit provided an excellent opportunity for research. He began to think that perhaps coming here had been a good idea after all.

The first hint that something might be rotten in Denmark came on the fourth day of his stay at Corbin Hall. That morning, a sorcerer demonstrated his improved method for removing stains from fabric. A few of the guests chuckled at this, or exchanged amused glances, as if they thought it a waste of time.

Peregrine, on the other hand, took detailed notes. He'd heard Abigail and Susan complain about the challenges of keeping table linens and clothing white, and he knew that such domestic magic was nothing to sneeze at. Abigail, being a witch, could not work sorcery, but Dora could. She might be glad to learn of a good housekeeping spell.

The second presentation, however, unsettled Peregrine. A wizard named Mr. Turnbull shared an improved method for drying horehound, mint, and catnip for use in spells. Rather than allowing the herbs to air-dry over a period of a few days, or exposing them to heat that might corrupt their magical properties, the excess water was removed through a dehydration spell. It was a simple, practical trick that Mr. Turnbull claimed would improve the magical and medicinal potency of the herbs. As such, it might be important to the thousands of British witches and wizards who used herbs in their spellcasting.

The problem was that Peregrine was certain he'd already heard about this technique for drying herbs. Hadn't Lady Markham told him about it? He furrowed his brow and bit his lip, trying to remember.

Yes, it had come up at Lord Kellway's dinner party a few weeks ago. Lady Markham had told Peregrine about brewing medicinal potions for the charitable dispensary she'd established near her husband's estate. She was a green witch who grew and harvested her own herbs, and he was sure she had mentioned a new method she'd learned for persevering horehound and mint. According to Lady Markham, herbs dried this way were more effective in healing teas and tinctures.

Peregrine could not be certain, but he thought the technique Mr. Turnbull described was identical to the one Lady Markham used. But Lady Markham had said she learned this method of drying herbs from a witch who lived in Lancashire, not a wizard from Northumberland. Peregrine did not see how to reconcile her story with Mr. Turnbull's presentation, and the discrepancy troubled him.

Peregrine waited politely for the question-and-answer period. "Did you by any chance learn this method from someone else?" he asked Mr. Turnbull. "I believe I have heard about a similar dehydration spell from a green witch I know."

Mr. Turnbull smiled benevolently. "As you know, Mr. Carrington, most spells and techniques have many regional variations. No doubt there are many similar tricks to drying herbs. But to the best of my knowledge, no one else has published anything about this specific method of preserving members of the mint family."

Peregrine frowned. "That does not quite speak to my question. I did not ask whether anyone had *published* this technique. I merely asked if someone else *developed* it. Did you learn it from someone else?" There would was no shame in Mr. Turnbull sharing a technique he had learned from another magician, provided he gave credit to the inventor.

A silence fell over the room, and Mr. Turnbull's smile faded. As Peregrine waited for his answer, he gradually became aware that other magicians were exchanging meaningful glances with each other. He scanned the room, feeling distinctly uneasy. Was it his imagination, or were some people staring in his direction?

Peregrine played with his pencil nervously. "I am sorry if I misspoke," he said at last. "I was merely curious." The uncomfortable silence suggested he had erred in some way, though he could see nothing wrong with what he'd said.

"Given how many different approaches there are to tending and harvesting herbs, it is not all impossible that someone else independently discovered this same method. But I assure you, I developed this technique entirely on my own." This time, Mr. Turnbull's toothy smile did not reach his eyes.

"I see. That makes sense." Peregrine's uneasiness had not been assuaged, but he wanted to smooth over the awkwardness in the room. To his relief, it worked. A few other magicians asked Mr. Turnbull questions. Then the party broke up for their afternoon recreation.

But Peregrine did not stop thinking about Turnbull's presentation. That afternoon, instead of researching in the library, he wrote a quick letter to Lady Markham, asking about the provenance of her technique for drying herbs. She would probably be surprised by the inquiry, since the two of them were not on such close terms as to correspond with each other. But he trusted her to answer his question honestly.

Perhaps he'd misunderstood or misremembered what Lady Markham had said about her method of preserving herbs. Perhaps there was some explanation for why Mr. Turnbull claimed to have invented a technique that Peregrine thought had been developed by a country hedgewitch. He hoped that was the case, because if not, Mr. Turnbull must be behaving disgracefully.

Peregrine would hate to think badly of a member of this friendly group of magicians, but he hated even more the idea that Mr. Turnbull might be doing something underhanded or dishonest. A *true* scholar always gave credit where credit was due. He could not approve of any magician who did not follow that rule.

CHAPTER THIRTEEN

"I AM VERY sorry, miss," the butler said, "but Lord Kellway is out. If you give me your card, I will see that he gets it."

"I do not have a card." Dora's shoulders slumped with despair. She had forgotten to put her card case in her reticule. The reticule was small, and the card case took up too much room, so she did not always carry it with her. A failure on her part, she now realized, but it was too late to do anything about it.

She eyed the butler speculatively. "Is Lord Kellway really out? Or is he merely not available to *me*?" She knew perfectly well that she was not supposed to ask such questions, but she couldn't help wondering.

A good butler was not supposed to show emotion, but the corners of this man's mouth turned down ever so slightly. "I cannot say, miss." Disapproval dripped from his voice.

That had to be a lie. The butler would know whether or not his employer was at home. It was his job to know such things!

Dora frowned. Should she remind the butler that she was Lord Valance's sister-in-law? She disliked relying on his title to earn respect, but there could be no denying that her social standing had improved now that she lived in the care of Lord and Lady Valance. As a viscountess, Honora could sponsor Dora into social circles beyond Lady Grantly's touch.

How Lady Grantly must *hate* that! It must be galling for the baronetess to realize that the illegitimate daughter of a concert singer could attend private balls and soirees to which Lady Grantly herself would never be invited. Perhaps it was wrong for Dora to take pleasure in such irony, but if so, she was willing to do wrong. After years of subtle snubs, seemingly accidental exclusions, and occasional blunt insults, Dora treasured even the smallest victory over her father's wife.

Before she could make up her mind whether to press the issue, the butler stepped back into the vestibule and began to close the door.

"Wait! Will you at least tell Lord Kellway that I called?" Why had she forgotten her calling cards? She didn't trust this disapproving servant to relay her message.

"Of course, miss." But he did not meet her eyes as he closed the door. All she heard in his voice was dismissal.

Damn. She clenched her jaw tightly. She had botched this. She ought to have brought Honora with her, rather than a footman. But Honora had wanted an afternoon nap, and Dora did not want to disturb her. She increasingly suspected that her sister was in a particularly delicate state of health at the moment.

Dora glanced back over her shoulder at the footman who had accompanied her. He stood rigidly by the curb, looking away from her. Pretending he hadn't just heard the butler unceremoniously turning her away. Very polite of him, she had to admit.

"We may as well go home, William." She deliberately unclenched her hands and jaw. She would simply have to call again tomorrow—and remember to bring her calling cards. Maybe next time she ought to wait until after her sister's nap, so Honora could accompany her.

To her surprise, William argued. "Wait a moment, Miss Rossini. I believe that is Lord Kellway's carriage coming up the lane now."

Dora hadn't paid any attention to the stately town coach approaching them. She was not particularly interested in carriages, and she certainly did not recognize the coats of arms of most members of the *ton*. But William had been in service for a few years, and he undoubtedly knew London society better than she did.

He was right. The carriage rolled to a stop right in front of Kellway House, and when the groom opened the door, His Lordship stepped out. This was her chance, then. She met Lord Kellway at the foot of the steps.

"Miss Rossini?" He inclined his head, though the wrinkle on his brow suggested that her presence outside his house confused him.

Dora curtseyed, hoping she correctly judged the necessary depth. There were fine gradations of obeisance for each level of the aristocracy. Lord Kellway was a baron, which put him at the bottom of the order of precedence for nobility, but still far above Dora.

"Were you calling on Lady Kellway? I believe she is out today. Tuesday is her day at home, you know."

His face looked open and friendly, encouraging her to hope that he would hear her out rather than brushing her aside. "No, my lord," Dora said. "I called hoping to speak to *you*."

"Indeed?" He raised his eyebrows. "To what do I owe the honor?"

Dora drew a deep breath. "It is about a letter which you sent to Mr. Carrington. He asked me to monitor his correspondence while he is away, so I was the one who read it, and I had some questions to ask before I forwarded it to—Mr. Carrington." She nearly slipped up and called him Peregrine, but she caught herself in time.

His gaze sharpened. "Ah," he said softly. "If you wish to discuss that, we had better speak in private. Will you step inside for a moment?"

"Yes, of course." She sagged with relief, knowing her errand would not be in vain after all. Then she forced herself to stand up straight and smile politely as she walked into the house beside Lord Kellway.

Dora felt a powerful temptation to smirk at the butler as he held the door open for them, but she resisted it. She did not want to cause insult in this household. That would not be for Peregrine's benefit in the long run, satisfying though it might feel at the moment.

Lord Kellway led her to his study, which was a fascinating room. She had expected to see walls lined with books. Most of the people in Peregrine's social circle collected books the way a white garment collected black cat hair. But though Kellway's study contained a few bookshelves, most of the cabinets lining the walls had been set up as display cases.

"Are those fossils?" she guessed, trying to remember what she'd heard about Lord Kellway and fossils.

"Yes, mostly ammonites and ancient fish. I specialize in marine fossils, you see. But there are some other fossils, too. This one is my most recent acquisition." He gestured to a glass case set at coffee-table level.

Dora looked down and gasped. A set of footprints marched across a flat stone. Printed as clearly as if they'd been made yesterday, they looked like bird footprints, though they were larger than chicken prints.

"What creature made those?" A turkey, perhaps? Or peafowl? Probably not an ostrich, she guessed. She'd never seen a live ostrich, but she assumed their footprints were larger than these.

"That is the question, isn't it?" The happy lilt in Lord Kellway's voice suggested that nothing in life brought him more joy than speculating about ancient lifeforms. Perhaps nothing did. "Some of my colleagues in the Royal Society of Geologic Magicians are trying to develop scrying techniques to look into the past to see the origin of the fossils, but so far, no one has been successful."

"Can scrying magic see into a different time?" Dora asked, surprised. She thought the only magic that could do that was divination, and she had never heard of divination that looked into the past rather than the future.

A magical spell that could reveal what had happened in the

past would completely transform the work of historians. It would be of considerable forensic importance, too. Murder trials would never be the same again—unless, of course, such magic was as unreliable as predictions of the future. Divination only produced future possibilities, not certainties.

"Seemingly not," Lord Kellway said. "But that does not stop people from trying. Maybe someday, someone will figure it out, and we will learn who made these tracks. I do not expect to live to see that day, but perhaps my grandchildren will." He lifted his eyes from the case and smiled at Dora. "But I doubt you came here to talk about fossils, Miss Rossini. Your tastes lie among the stars rather than in the earth, don't they?"

"I am interested in many different types of magic. I have not yet settled on a specialty. What I really like is a challenge."

Peregrine's meteorite trap, being the most intricate bit of spellcasting she had ever encountered, had immediately caught her fancy. But the magic itself intrigued her more than the meteorites. She enjoyed collaborating with Peregrine, but she would probably have enjoyed it just as much if he pursued an equally complex alternative subject.

She glanced back down at the display case, wondering again what had left those footprints. "If I had world enough and time, I would love to learn more about geological magic, but—" She shrugged.

To her surprise, Lord Kellway chuckled. "I suspect you will have decades ahead of you in which to pursue the study of magic. You are, if you will forgive my saying so, quite young, Miss Rossini. Those of us who are past the prime of life may worry about time's winged chariot hurrying near, but I doubt you have any reason to fear it. But"—his smile fell—"you said you came to talk about a letter I sent?"

"Yes." Dora stood up straighter, lifting her eyes away from the display case. Best to get right to the point. "You wrote to Mr. Carrington, warning him not to trust Mr. Blithfield. Why?"

Lord Kellway flinched at her bluntness. "I am afraid I cannot yet reveal the cause of my concerns, but I assure you that Mr. Carrington would do well to give Blithfield a wide berth."

"It is a bit late for that." Dora's voice sounded crisp, calm, and confident, though her heart pounded more quickly. Was Peregrine in some kind of danger? "Your letter was delayed, so Mr. Carrington did not receive your warning in time. He is already at Corbin Hall, attending a house party hosted by Mr. Blithfield."

Lord Kellway's face went blank. He shifted his eyes away from her, looking into the distance. "I had not realized that. That is most unfortunate." He frowned as he turned back to Dora. "Thank you for letting me know, Miss Rossini. You had better forward that letter to Mr. Carrington. And I will do my best to contact him as well . . . though"—he frowned—"I do not want to give anything away to Mr. Blithfield."

"Give anything away?" Dora tipped her head to one side. Curiosity mingled with concern.

"I do not want Blithfield to know that I have been investigating him," Lord Kellway explained. "As of now, I lack sufficient evidence to take any kind of action against him. It would be best if he had no idea that I warned Mr. Carrington."

"Oh, I can take care of that." Dora waved away his concern. "I can transport a letter directly to Peregrine. No one else in the house need ever know." The spell she'd perfected working with Valance was already proving useful!

Lord Kellway nodded. "Yes, you had better do that. In the meantime, I will contact a magician I know in Carlisle and ask him to keep an eye out for any trouble at Corbin Hall."

"Will that be enough to keep Peregrine safe?" This time, Dora's control slipped, and some of her anxiety seeped into her voice. She could not help wondering what kind of "trouble" Lord Kellway envisioned.

"He is in no *physical* danger," Lord Kellway assured her. "I have no reason to believe that either Blithfield or his colleagues are violent. The situation is much more complicated, and the threat they pose is more subtle."

That was all he would say. Though Dora had many questions, she was given no opportunity to ask them. Instead, Lord Kellway escorted her to the vestibule, where she found her footman patiently waiting.

"We had better go home, William," she said. He nodded and followed her out the door.

It was, unfortunately, raining again, and once again she had not thought to bring an umbrella. She really ought to have learned her lesson by now!

"Do you want me to find a hack for you?" William suggested. "Or run home for an umbrella?"

"No, thank you." Dora shuddered at the very idea. Did none of the aristocracy show any consideration for their servants? "Either way, *you* would get rained on, so why shouldn't I get wet, too? A little rain won't hurt me."

Long before she reached Curzon Street, she discovered that this was more than a *little* rain. But she stood by her decision. It would not be right to force William to make extra trips back and forth merely in order to keep her dry. His comfort was no less important than hers.

Once she got home, though, she was quite happy to change her wet clothes for dry ones. She rang for the lady's maid she shared with her sister. Just before Clack entered the room, Dora noticed a rather grubby, crumpled-looking letter on her dressing table. That childish print could only be Jack's handwriting! A smile tugged at the corner of her lips, but she had to wait to read the letter while Clack fussed over her damp hair.

She sat not-very-patiently while Clack simultaneously combed her hair and delivered a lecture about how young ladies ought not go walking in the rain without an umbrella. As soon as the maid left the room, Dora broke open the letter.

Dear Dora,

I am very glad to hear from you! Mama says you are going to come to some bad end, but I bet you are having an adventure. I wish you had taken me along with you when you ran away. I miss you and Honora. Belinda refuses to play with Clarinda and me the way you used to do. She says she is too old for that!

Are you ever going to come home? If you are, you better come home soon, because next year I will be away at school. I thought I would go to Ashton Academy when I turned thirteen, like Papa did, but Mama says Westminster is cheaper, and they accept little boys, not just big ones. If I go to Westminster, do you think you and Honora can visit sometimes? Belinda and Clarinda will not be going to school next year. Miss Merton's academy is too expensive.

I wish you were here to explain my magic lesson to me. You were better at answering my questions than Mr. Rhodes. Most of the time he just says, "You will better understand when you are older, Sir Jacob." But I don't want to understand it when I am older. I want to understand it now!

I have to go, Mama keeps asking what I'm scribbling about and I am running out of answers. Love from me and Clarinda!

Your brother,
Jack

Dora did not cry after reading the letter; she was not prone to tears. But she did have to swallow heavily to cope with the sudden lump in her throat. She could practically hear Jack's light, boyish voice saying all of that—just as she could hear Belinda insisting that she was "too old" to play with her younger siblings. Belinda desperately wanted to be a young lady, go to balls, and flirt with gentlemen.

Unfortunately, she could also too easily imagine Lady Grantly predicting that Dora would "come to some bad end." Bless Jack for refusing to believe that! He deserved a better mother than Lady Grantly. They all did.

Well, there was nothing Dora could do to give her younger siblings the parents they deserved. But there might be something she could do about Peregrine's situation.

She would forward the letter to Peregrine, of course, using the sending spell she'd already perfected. But would that be enough? Or ought she take some additional action? An idea began to percolate through her brain. Her brother-in-law would not like it, she knew that much. But he was not her legal guardian, so he did not have the authority to stop her, did he? And Dora felt certain that her sister would understand.

Was it necessary to go to such an extreme? She took time to give the question due consideration. She had been told in no uncertain terms that she needed to avoid scandal, since that might weaken the Chancery case against the Grantlys. Her very future depended on it, since she needed her guardian's permission to marry. That did give her pause.

But there must be a way to help Peregrine without getting caught in scandal. The Season was winding down, so it wouldn't seem suspicious if Dora stopped attending social events. She could claim to have an illness that kept her at home. . . no one would bother to verify that. Dora knew she could rely on her sister to cover for her.

Besides, Peregrine's well-being was far more important than Dora's reputation. He was a capable adult and he was at home in the world of magicians, but anyone might need help in a case like this. Who else was likely to ride to his aid? No one, that's who. And if rushing to Peregrine's aid added a little zest to Dora's life, well, that was all for the good. Despite what her younger brother imagined, Dora felt a distinct lack of adventure at the moment.

Time to stir up a little trouble, she decided. For a good cause, of course! She smiled at her reflection in the mirror, and the reflection grinned mischievously back.

CHAPTER FOURTEEN

Peregrine found the letter when he went up to his guest room after dinner. It sat on top of the papers piled on the escritoire. He recognized the handwriting on the envelope immediately, but was surprised by the thickness of the packet. He was even more surprised when he opened Dora's letter to find a missive from Lord Kellway tucked inside.

Dora's note was brief and straight to the point. She wrote that the enclosed letter had somehow been delayed, that its contents seemed important, and that she loved Peregrine and hoped to see him soon. He already knew she loved him, and he too wished he could see her soon. Given that he still had more than a week before the house party ended, though, that seemed unlikely.

Lord Kellway's note was more perplexing. As Peregrine read it, his frown deepened. Mr. Blithfield was not worthy of his trust? In what way? He uneasily wondered whether the warning had anything to do with Mr. Turnbull's presentation yesterday. Surely not. . . but he found himself asking whether he ought to make his excuses and leave the house party now.

But he had yet to hear from Lady Markham about her technique for drying herbs, and he did not like abandoning a mystery before it was solved. Surely it would not hurt to stay until he heard back from Lady Markham?

Still, he decided it might be wise to prepare in case he did need to leave in a hurry. He scratched out a quick note to Dora, letting her know that he intended to stay for now, but would cut his visit short if need arose. Then he stared at the note for a long moment. Should he mention the strange matter of Mr. Turnbull's presentation?

No, he decided. His concerns were so vague, they were not even worth calling suspicions. It might still be pure coincidence that Turnbull had developed a technique similar to the one Lady Markham learned in Lancashire. Or Peregrine's own memory might have been at fault. When all was said and done, Peregrine had no evidence of wrongdoing. Even if Mr. Turnball *was* guilty of dishonesty, it did not follow that his misconduct was at all connected to Lord Kellway's warning.

Rather than saying anything about the troubling presentation, Peregrine concluded his brief letter with a question about the Valances' plans for after the Season ended. Then he set the letter aside to mail later. Being a wizard rather than a sorcerer, he could not work the same sending spell Dora used. His version required eyebright and oak gall, and he was out of both ingredients. He would have to go into town for more supplies.

HE COULDN'T HAVE chosen a better day for a solitary ride into Carlisle. Clouds piling up in the distance suggested rain might be on the way, but for now, the sun shone brightly, birds sang, and the only thing Peregrine had to worry about was the tendency of his borrowed horse to snatch mouthfuls of grass from the side of the road.

"I would think that they didn't feed you enough," Peregrine told his mount, "but you don't seem to be wasting away." The bay gelding was big boned and well-muscled—clearly not as underfed as his constant snacking might suggest.

The horse snorted, but he grudgingly lifted his head and resumed his lazy walk. It did not seem possible to bestir him to a trot, so Peregrine resigned himself to a long, slow ride into town. The head groom at Corbin Hall must have misunderstood what he meant when he asked for a well-broke mount. Next time, he would make it clear that he could handle something a little more spirited than a rocking horse.

Peregrine had never been to Carlisle before, but it was easy enough to find an inn where he could leave his horse while he shopped.

Some of the shops were doing a bustling trade, but Beck's Magical Emporium was nearly empty. There were only two other customers inside: a gray-haired gentleman and a woman of indeterminable age who was happily telling the gentleman her opinion on the best treatment for an upset stomach. She swore by peppermint rather than ginger and had a complicated theory as to why it was more effective.

Peregrine tried to tune out the conversation while he put in his order. But it took time for the shopkeeper's assistant to gather and wrap up all the herbs and minerals Peregrine requested. In his boredom, Peregrine stole an occasional glance at the voluble healer. This was a mistake, for she caught his eye and mistook his idle curiosity for an invitation to chat.

"And who might you be, young man?" She smiled, revealing a missing tooth. "For I've not seen you here before, and I know all the magicians in town. Aye, and most of them in the county, for that matter, what with having lived here my whole life."

"I am a guest at Corbin Hall, visiting Mr. Blithfield." Peregrine was uncomfortable with the way she had approached him without a proper introduction, but that was no reason to be rude to her.

"Oh, that's right," she agreed. "The big house is full of magicians just now, isn't it? Wizards and mages and sorcerers, oh my! Mr. Blithfield does like to entertain magical gentlemen. And where are you from, then? For I am sure you are not from hereabouts."

"I am from Surrey." Much to his relief, the shopkeeper's

assistant returned with all of Peregrine's requested materials, giving him an excuse to duck out of the conversation. He paid for his purchases, tucked the brown-paper bundle under his arm, and turned to leave.

"Excuse me, young man." Much to his surprise, the gray-haired gentleman stepped in front of him. "I heard that you were from Surrey?"

"Yes?" Peregrine cautiously replied. Were all the inhabitants of this town overly inquisitive? There should be nothing remarkable about his being from Surrey. That county's proximity to London meant it attracted more than the usual number of magicians. He could hardly be the only one who occasionally traveled to the north of England.

"Forgive me for presuming," the gentleman said, "might you, by any chance, be Mr. Carrington?"

Peregrine took a step backward in surprise. "Yes, I am. But how did you know that? We have not met, have we? Or are you a member of my club?" There were many country gentlemen who joined the Cambion Club but rarely came to town. He could not keep track of all of them.

"No." The stranger dismissed that suggestion with a shake of his head. "I rarely come to London. But I believe we have an acquaintance in common. Lord Kellway asked me to look out for you."

"Oh, is that so?" Peregrine felt baffled as to why Lord Kellway would want anyone to look out for him. He was not a child, and he was perfectly capable of taking care of himself.

"Ah, yes, I ought to let you know who I am." The gentleman handed Peregrine a card that read "E. Mattinson, General Practice Wizardry."

That still left Peregrine with questions about why Mr. Mattinson had taken the liberty of introducing himself. "It is a pleasure to meet you, Mr. Mattinson. May I be of service in some way?"

"Oh, not at all. But if ever *you* need assistance of any kind, please do feel free to call upon me." Mr. Mattinson dropped his voice to a whisper as he said: "I am afraid that Mr. Blithfield is not the safest acquaintance for an inventive young magician."

Ah, so that's what this was about. Peregrine relaxed slightly. "I have received Lord Kellway's warning on that subject." He did not quite whisper, but he did lower his voice. "I assure you, I shall be on my guard." Though he did not yet know what, precisely, he should be on his guard against.

"Very well. Good day, Mr. Carrington." Mr. Mattinson nodded his head and turned to talk to the man behind the counter. Peregrine hurried out the door. He wanted to return to Corbin Hall and work his sending spell right away, before anyone could distract him.

But when he returned from his ride, sunburnt and tired, he could not find the letter he'd written for Dora. He remembered quite clearly leaving it on the escritoire, but there was nothing there. Puzzled, he rang for a maid.

"Do you know what happened to the letter I left here?" He tapped the precise place where he'd left it.

The maid bobbed her head. "Oh, yes, sir. I brought it down and put it on the tray with the other mail. The letter carrier will pick it up tomorrow morning."

Peregrine's lips tightened. The housemaids could not have known that he intended to send the letter through magic rather than via the postal service, but they might at least have asked before taking it! He cleared his throat to buy himself time to get his temper under control.

"Ah, thank you. But in the future, please do not remove any of my correspondence, for any reason."

"Yes, sir." The maid bobbed her head again and scurried away, looking thoroughly chastened.

Peregrine assumed his letter would still be in the mail tray in the front hall. It would have been placed there after the post had already been picked up for the day. But when he rifled through the letters stacked on the silver tray, his letter was nowhere to be found.

"May I help you, Mr. Carrington?" The butler spoke politely, but Peregrine felt like a naughty child caught in the middle of wrongdoing. Going through other people's mail probably looked suspicious.

"I merely wondered what happened to a letter I intended to post. Because it is not here. But it should be. And I want it back." He knew he was babbling, but he had no idea how to explain all the complications and nuances of the situation. Strictly speaking, he had not intended to *post* that letter at all, since it would be far faster to send it by magic rather than by mail coach.

"Sir," the butler said gently, "if your letter is not there now, it must have been picked up with the rest of the post earlier today."

Peregrine shook his head. "No, it was set out too late. I'm sure . . ." He paused, rethinking that. *Was* he certain it had not been picked up with today's post? He might very well be wrong about the hour when the post had been picked up. "I thought it was put out too late for that."

"If it is not there," the butler repeated, "it is on its way to the recipient. Is there anything else I can help you with, sir?"

"No, thank you." He walked away, feeling defeated.

Something about this situation both confused and troubled him, but he could not put his finger on what exactly was wrong. Maybe the letter really had been posted properly. Surely that was more likely than that someone would have stolen his letter? But then again, both Lord Kellway and Mr. Mattinson had warned Peregrine not to trust Mr. Blithfield. Peregrine could not dismiss the possibility that his letter had been stolen for some unknown reason.

Just in case the letter had gone astray, he wrote a new one to Dora, outlining his concerns and the possibility that he might leave the house party earlier than anticipated. And then, though he felt a little paranoid, he told her about the missing letter and his fear that it might have been stolen or detained by someone in the house.

Peregrine did not wait to send this second letter. He did not even leave the room. Though the billiard room had been equipped as a temporary laboratory for the use of visiting wizards, this spell was simple enough that Peregrine could work it in the privacy of his own room, using tools from his magic kit.

Peregrine's version of the sending spell required grinding up the requisite herbs, burning them over a spirit lamp, then chanting the Latin words of the spell while he patiently held the envelope above the smoking concoction. He poured magic into every word until the spell "caught" and the letter vanished, leaving only a draft of air.

The moment the letter disappeared, some of his tension drained away. He had done all he could. Dora would get the letter immediately, and she might even be able to respond today. That possibility comforted him, and he went down to dinner in a much better mood. Perhaps there would be a response waiting for him after dinner.

BUT NO REPLY awaited him when he turned in for the night. No letter arrived from Dora the next day, or the day after that. That seemed odd, because Dora was a much more reliable correspondent than Peregrine himself. He was not usually the one left waiting for a response. But perhaps her time was taken up with the last social events of the Season. He ought to hear from her soon enough, he told himself. In any case, less than a week remained of this blasted house party, so he would see her in person soon enough.

He did, however, get a reply from Lady Markham. She did remember the conversation they'd had about quickly drying herbs with magic. She used that method regularly, she explained, because it was faster and resulted in a stronger potion.

Moreover, Lady Markham very clearly remembered learning

this method no more than a year ago, from a local herbwoman she met after moving to Lancashire. Goody Enfield had developed the practice after getting frustrated with the way fresh herbs lost their potency during the long, slow air-drying process. So far as Lady Markham knew, the only magicians who knew about the technique were local witches and herbwomen who had learned it from Mrs. Enfield herself.

Best of all, she enclosed a second sheet of paper with detailed instruction on how to dry herbs Goody Enfield's way. Peregrine scanned it carefully. To all appearances, it seemed identical to the method described by Mr. Turnbull. But he did not need to rely on his memory. He pulled out his notebook and flipped pages until he found the notes from that day.

Yes, both the list of ingredients and the proportions of them were the same. The directions were worded differently, but he supposed that was to be expected. The incantation Mr. Turnbull had shared was in Latin, whereas Goody Enfield's was in English, but when the Latin was translated into English, the spells were nearly identical.

It was, of course, possible for two magicians to independently develop very similar spells, as Mr. Turnbull had pointed out. But if that were the case, one would expect a few small differences: golden thyme rather than regular thyme, for example, or a slightly different incantation. There were no such minor differences between these two spells. The similarities were, in Peregrine's very educated opinion, too strong to be coincidental.

So, there it was in black and white: Someone had developed the quick-drying spell before Mr. Turnbull. It appeared that Mr. Turnbull had lied about the spell's origins. He had presented as his own work a spell that had actually been developed by a country herbwoman—a woman who probably earned less than a tenth of Mr. Turnbull's income, though she might have decades more practical experience.

Peregrine did not often lose his temper. When people confused him, he did his best to understand why they might have behaved differently than he would have. His father had taught him to extend the principle of charity and assume the best about other people, whether or not they extended the same courtesy to him.

But the more he thought about this theft (for it was a theft, albeit a theft of ideas rather than objects), the angrier he grew. A true gentleman would never take credit for someone else's work. It was particularly ungentlemanly to steal an idea from a woman of lower social standing. Mrs. Enfield's magic practice might have benefited from recognition of her work. Mr. Turnbull's behavior was more than merely unsporting. It was unethical, and it ought to get him disbarred from any professional magical organization.

Given the letter from Lord Kellway, there might be an even bigger problem at Corbin Hall. Lord Kellway had warned Peregrine against the host of the house party, not the guests. Did that imply that Mr. Blithfield knew about the dishonesty? Peregrine stayed up late into the night pondering that question, without ever coming to an answer.

CHAPTER FIFTEEN

ORIGINALLY, DORA PLANNED to tell her older sister before she snuck out of London in disguise. Honora might not be her legal guardian, but she was one of the few relatives whose opinion Dora respected. Unlike the guardians who tried to control Dora's life, Honora actually cared about Dora's well-being. Honora, moreover, had done some outrageously unconventional things in the past (admittedly not as often as Dora). Honora probably would not like Dora traveling alone, but she was unlikely to stop her from doing it.

But Dora felt certain that her brother-in-law would object to her traveling to Cumberland on her own, no matter what clothing she wore. And it did not seem quite good form to ask Honora to keep a secret from her own husband. Dora did not want to create any tension between the two. Better to tell neither of the Valances about her plan in advance.

She would simply leave a note for them; that would be the courteous thing to do. But, to make certain that no one could interfere with her plan, she cast a temporary concealment spell on the note. It should stay hidden for at least a day. By the time anyone could see the note, she would have gotten a solid head start. Hopefully she would make it Corbin Hall before anyone caught up with her—assuming that anyone even tried to do so.

Dora had traveled on a public stagecoach before, and she'd enjoyed it. But her trip from rural Kent into London took less than a full day. Maintaining her disguise as a boy had not been terribly hard, but she had not had to do it for very long. This trip would be different: It took days to get to Cumberland.

She had never tried to pass herself off as Theo Rossini for more than a day. Passing as a young man involved more than just a change of dress. Theo Rossini used different slang than Dora, talked in a different register, and moved in quite different ways. Maintaining that identity for days would be a challenge.

But Dora liked a good challenge—and she had found life in London rather stale since Peregrine left. She looked forward to surprising him. If a little voice at the back of her mind hinted that Peregrine did not particularly *like* surprises, she refused to listen to it. He would like seeing *her* again. She could be certain of that.

Her journey began with an incredible piece of luck: a space opened up on the Royal Mail, due to a passenger's sudden illness. It would take her less than three days to travel from London to Carlisle, because the mail coach traveled by night. She snagged a corner seat, squished between a snoozing farmer's wife and the wall of the coach, and prepared for adventure.

ALAS, ADVENTURE DID not answer her summons. Instead, Dora spent hours being uncomfortably bounced around. When night fell, everyone in the coach slept as best they could, so there were no interesting conversations to be had. But Dora did not repine. She rested her head against the padded wall and fell sound asleep, though she woke every time the coach stopped to change horses.

In the morning, there was time only to grab a cup of tea and a roll. She realized, belatedly, that she ought to have packed food for herself. She had never ridden on the mail coach before and had not realized how short the stops were. The mail stopped for only as long as it took to change horses, and that took only a few minutes, making it difficult to use the necessary or purchase food.

Once day dawned and the passengers woke up, she began to learn more about them. The passenger next to her was an elderly woman named Mrs. Bewley. She was returning home after caring for her married daughter, who had just given birth to her eighth child ("but only five living, poor thing").

Dora's eyes widened as she listened to a lengthy and graphic account of the birth. By the end of the story, she felt extremely grateful for the existence of contraceptive magic. She marveled that her sister was willing to experience such an ordeal. Of course Honora, being married to a wealthy nobleman, could afford the best medical care. Perhaps that made a difference. Dora certainly hoped it did, for her sister's sake.

The other occupants inside the coach included a girl who looked about Dora's age, or possibly a little younger, and a fair-haired boy who looked like he ought to be up at university, since Trinity term had not yet ended. The young lady had blue eyes and dark-brown hair, and she was very fashionably dressed, though she traveled without a maid or chaperone.

Initially, the young lady and the young gentleman seemed not to know one another. At least, they never spoke to each other. But anytime Mrs. Bewley said something shocking or amusing, their eyes would meet and they would smile, as if they shared a private joke.

When the young lady—she said her name was Miss Smith— shivered and complained of the cold, the young gentleman—he said his name was Jones—offered her his greatcoat. That could have been mere gallantry, but Dora, piecing together the puzzling interactions, began to suspect that the young people knew each other better than they let on.

Unlikely though it might be, Dora suspected she wasn't the only passenger traveling under a pseudonym. She would have dearly loved to hear Miss Smith and Mr. Jones's story, but she knew better than to press for details. If they had reason to travel incognito, she ought to respect their privacy. (She certainly hoped that others would treat her the same way.)

So, she contented herself with imagining possible scenarios to account for their deception. Being possessed of a powerful imagination, she kept herself well entertained this way.

ADVENTURE DID NOT strike until the second morning on the road. All four of the inside passengers remained on the coach, though two of the outside passengers had disembarked at one of the stops. Mrs. Bewley, having exhausted all of her stories of painful and dramatic childbirth, began talking about deathbeds instead—though, indeed, the two subjects often overlapped.

Dora listened patiently while her traveling companion described all of the many symptoms of her sister's final, fatal illness. The identity of the illness remained unclear, as it combined the effects of dropsy, consumption, and brain fever. Mrs. Bewley seemed proud that her sister had managed to stump both the apothecary and the surgeon who were called in to attend her.

"I suppose if you have to die, you might as well die with some flair," Dora said doubtfully. She wasn't convinced that confounding the medical establishment was adequate compensation for being forced to shuffle off this mortal coil.

Before Mrs. Bewley could respond, a blast of the coachman's horn commanded everyone's attention. Dora initially assumed it was a signal to the keeper at a tollgate, but shouting and profanity followed a moment later. The coachman's language grew increasingly coarse as the coach slowed and came to a halt.

"Such shocking language!" Though she shook her head, Mrs. Bewley did not sound at all perturbed. If anything, she seemed to relish the prospect of an interruption to their tedious journey.

Dora struggled to listen in on the conversation outside the coach, but all she knew for certain was that someone had blocked the road. When she looked past the profanity in the coachman's speech, she concluded that he was threatening someone with legal prosecution for obstructing the king's highway.

"*Is* it against the law to block the road?" Dora wondered aloud.

"Probably. Oh, I do hope it is not a highwayman!" Both Mrs. Bewley's eager tone and the way she peered out the window suggested she would welcome the drama of a highwayman.

Dora sympathized, but she also worried. A little stand-and-deliver might seem very entertaining, but she did not want anyone to take her money. If her pockets were to let, making her way to Carlisle might be difficult, if not disastrous.

She leaned back against the squabs and rapidly reviewed all the defensive magic she knew. The basic shielding spell would protect her from gunfire, but it might not stand up to magical force if she were attacked by someone who had more experience with combat magic.

"A highwayman?" Miss Smith's face turned white, and her hands tightened around the handle of her hatbox.

"You need not fear," Mr. Jones assured her. "I will protect you. I mean, all of you." He looked across the carriage at Dora and Mrs. Bewley, as if he'd meant to include them all along.

Dora felt fairly certain that he had, in fact, meant he would specifically protect Miss Smith. Her suspicions were confirmed when Mr. Jones surreptitiously took Miss Smith's hand. Miss Smith, far from protesting this intrusion, looked up at him and smiled faintly.

Sweethearts, Dora thought. There could be no doubt. Then why did they pretend not to know each other? Not that they were doing a good job of maintaining the ruse. But still, why did they think they needed to pretend at all?

Her speculation was cut short when someone threw open the door of the coach. A young man with dark-brown hair and impressive side whiskers glared into the coach. "Emily!" he snapped.

Miss Smith flinched. "Gabriel! What are you doing here?"

"Do you have any idea how worried Mother and Father have

been?" the intruder demanded.

Her brother, then, Dora concluded. Now that she thought about it, she could see a resemblance in the shape of their noses. She flicked her eyes towards Mr. Jones. He had wrapped one arm defensively about Miss Smith, or whatever her real name was.

"Emily is not going back with you!" Mr. Jones announced. "She will not be forced into marrying that wastrel!"

Gabriel rolled his eyes. "No one is trying to force her to do anything," he grumbled. "But she is a minor. She must come back home. And you, sir, ought to be horsewhipped." He glowered at Mr. Jones.

"I always did love an elopement," Mrs. Bewley confided to Dora. "So romantic!" She beamed at the young couple.

Dora nodded, not so much because she thought it was romantic as because she agreed with Mrs. Bewley's assessment of the situation. Emily What's-Her-Name must be eloping with Mr. Jones. Naturally, they would be headed north so they could marry across the border.

Gabriel turned his scowl toward Mrs. Bewley. "There is nothing romantic about a girl of eighteen stealing her own father's money out of a safe and bolting off to Scotland with a feckless stripling!"

Mr. Jones lunged forward. He might very well have planted his soon-to-be brother-in-law a facer if Emily had not pulled him back.

"Stop that, both of you!" Emily abandoned her frightened young miss act. "Gabriel, I am not going back home, and you cannot force me to do so!" She paced a hand over her heart as she made this noble declaration. She might well have been acting a scene on stage.

"We'll see about that." Her brother started to climb into the carriage, intent on retrieving his wayward sister.

Then two unexpected things happened almost simultaneously. First, the coach lurched forward as the horses resumed their trot northward.

Second, and rather more surprisingly, Mrs. Bewley announced "You aren't wanted here, young man!" She gave Gabriel a firm shove. He tumbled right out of the rolling coach, yelping as he hit the road.

Emily shrieked and covered her mouth with her hands. "My brother! You might have killed him!"

"He's probably just bruised," Mr. Jones assured her. "And dirty." He smiled, as if the prospect pleased him, but he wiped the smile off his face when Emily glowered at him. "I think we had better get off at the next stop and find alternative transportation," he suggested. "Now that he knows what coach we're on, it will be too easy to track us."

Frankly, Dora thought it would be easy to track them no matter what transportation they used. Had they even bothered to disguise their appearances? She suspected not. *Amateurs!*

"I am sure you are wondering what all that was about." Emily looked timidly across to where Dora and Mrs. Bewley sat.

The coach horses had by now resumed their former brisk trot, and everyone seemed to relax. Gabriel's tumble out of the coach would probably slow him down, even if he had not been seriously injured.

Dora did not wonder what "all that" had been about. She felt certain. "You are running off to Scotland to get married, aren't you?"

"Aye, that's plain enough!" Mrs. Bewley agreed. "And good for you, lass. Don't let them tell you what to do!"

"They only object because they think we are too young, anyway," Mr. Jones explained. "But we will show them! We—"

Dora interrupted what promised to be a lengthy speech. "You had better change your appearance somehow."

"Change our appearance?" Young Mr. Jones widened his eyes.

"Dye your hair. Or cut it." Dora turned to address Emily. "If you cropped your hair and dyed it, you would be harder to identify. And if you dressed in a working woman's clothing, no one would realize that you were a gentlewoman." Emily's refined speech might give her away, but maybe she could avoid talking.

"What?" Emily's jaw dropped. "I could never do that!"

But Mr. Jones looked at Dora with something like awe. "That's really quite clever. I am beholden to you for the suggestion."

"You're welcome." Dora leaned back against the squabs and closed her eyes, disappointed that the morning's adventure had already ended.

She still had all her gold in her pocket, true, but how would she entertain herself for the rest of the journey? Mrs. Bewley probably had an inexhaustible supply of gruesome medical stories, but by now, they had lost their appeal.

The young couple alighted from the mail coach at the next stop. Dora wished them good luck, though she would not have wagered much on their chance of escaping Emily's brother. They seemed not to have planned their elopement very well. Dora would have done a much better job if *she* had decided to run off with her young man!

She leaned her head against the side of the carriage, closed her eyes, and thought wistfully about eloping with Peregrine. Carlisle was very close to the border, wasn't it? Perhaps this journey could kill two birds with one stone. If she married, her Uncle Robert would no longer have any legal control over her, though he would still control the money held in trust for her. That rankled, but maybe Valance's solicitor would find out a way around it. According to Mr. Watson, replacing an unfit trustee was difficult, but not impossible.

The more Dora thought about marrying at the anvil, the more she liked the idea. An irregular marriage in Scotland would circumvent not only her guardians' restrictions, but also the English law that required Dora to marry in an Anglican church. One of the few things Dora knew about her life before her mother's death was that she had received a Roman Catholic baptism, not an Anglican one. She had seen the baptismal certificate with her own eyes.

After her mother's death, Dora had attended her father's church, but as she grew older, she came to view her father's decision to raise her in the Church of England as a rejection of her mother's culture. Dora knew little about Roman Catholicism and even less about her mother's personal religious beliefs, but she had chosen not to live as Anglican out of respect for the late Caterina Rossini. She refused to be confirmed, and once she left home, she avoided church altogether.

In England, Roman Catholics could not be legally married in their own churches, according to their own rites. Like most Dissenters, they were required to marry in an Anglican ceremony. Some English Catholics had a Catholic wedding after the Anglican one, but it was the Protestant ceremony that counted for legal purposes.

In Scotland, however, anyone could marry simply by declaring their intention to marry in front of witnesses. One need not step foot in a church at all. Dora liked the idea of thumbing her nose at English penal laws rather than conforming to them.

There would also be other, more carnal, advantages to matrimony. Dora smiled as she thought about the chance to do more than kiss the man she loved. Though she was inexperienced, she was not uneducated. Her older sister had done her best to explain the mechanics of what men and women did in bed, though Honora stubbornly refused to share personal details about her own experience as a married woman. Dora had done a little experimenting on her own, but that was hardly the same as sharing physical pleasure with someone else.

All she had to do was convince Peregrine. His older brother had asked him not to elope, but Dora doubted that Peregrine would refuse her request when they were already so close to the border. Once they were married, she would be out of Lady Grantly's control forever.

With that pleasing prospect in mind, she could listen patiently to Mrs. Bewley's tales of accidents and illnesses all the way to their destination.

CHAPTER SIXTEEN

T HE MYSTERY OF his disappearing letter nagged at the back of Peregrine's mind for the next few days. He could not quit thinking about it. Had it really been posted, or not? To make matters worse, he had yet to receive any kind of answer from Dora. Did that mean she hadn't gotten the letter, or simply that she hadn't had time to respond? So many frustrating possibilities!

It troubled him so much that he rode back into town to call on Mr. Mattinson. The wizard lived in a handsome town house on a respectable street, and a properly dignified butler answered the door. Either Mr. Mattinson had inherited an independent fortune or his wizarding practice had been unusually profitable.

The butler left Peregrine in a large parlor with heavy mahogany furniture. He perched in a somewhat uncomfortable chair near the open window, which let in both fresh air and the sounds of carriages rolling down the cobbled street.

When Mr. Mattinson entered the room, he initially seemed pleased to see Peregrine, but his smile fell as Peregrine explained what brought him there. He pulled a chair around to face Peregrine and listened patiently to the whole story.

"What could anyone gain by taking your letter?" he asked.

Peregrine sighed. It was a perfectly reasonable question, and he had no good answer for it. Stealing someone's private correspondence violated all principles of good manners and proper hospitality. Much as he loved Dora, he couldn't imagine anything in his letter to her that was important enough to make such a breach of etiquette worthwhile.

"If someone read the letter, they would know that I knew that Lord Kellway suspected Mr. Blithfield of. . . foul play." He shook his head, disliking his own wording. "I am sure that is putting it too strongly."

"I'm not so sure. *Foul play* may be exactly the right phrase." Mr. Mattinson took his spectacles off and wiped the lenses with his handkerchief. "I suppose I'd better explain the situation a little better, since you seem to already have become entangled in it."

"Yes, please do." Peregrine sat up straighter, hoping he was finally going to hear more than just mysterious hints.

"I don't know how much I am at liberty to say," his companion explained. "But Lord Kellway suspects Mr. Blithfield of intellectual dishonesty, and possibly misuse of magic."

"Misuse of magic?" Peregrine had already seen evidence of the intellectual dishonesty, but he had not seen any hint of *that*. Legal penalties for misusing magic could be quite stiff.

"Possibly," Mr. Mattinson cautioned. "I don't believe there is any clear evidence of that. But I spoke to Lord Kellway yesterday, and he—"

Peregrine frowned. "You spoke to him? Isn't he in London?"

Mr. Mattinson nodded. "Yes, but I have a gift for long-distance scrying. I can talk to someone through a mirror, though getting the attention of the person with whom I wish to communicate can be difficult. Most people ignore their mirror when they are not shaving or dressing, after all, so—but that is neither here nor there." Mr. Mattinson shook his head to dismiss the digression. "Suffice it to say that I spoke to Kellway yesterday, and he asked me to assist you if you ran into any trouble with Blithfield or his colleagues."

Any trouble, Peregrine thought. He hated how vague all these hints were. Why couldn't anyone spell out the nature of the trouble? What, exactly, did Lord Kellway fear Blithfield or his colleagues might do? He could only think of one likely possibility.

"You think they are going to . . . what? Steal a spell from me?"

"Possibly." Mr. Mattinson put his glasses back on and leaned back in his chair. "I hope our suspicions prove groundless, but yes, that is what Kellway and I fear. Rumor says that Blithfield and some of his colleagues are in the habit of taking other people's spells or techniques and claiming them as their own work."

Peregrine nodded. "I believe I have already seen some evidence of that during this house party. But I don't understand how Blithfield or his colleagues could be a threat to *me*. I am happy to share my work with anyone who wants to learn it. What could Blithfield gain from stealing information from me? And how could he claim it is his own work? I have already presented on the subject to the Society of Astronomical Magicians!" Blithfield knew about that presentation, because he'd been at the Society's annual meeting.

"But have you done any work on the spell *since* that presentation?" Mr. Mattinson studied him with keen eyes.

Peregrine lowered his gaze. "Well, yes, I have kept working on it." He had, as he told Mr. Blithfield, been trying to make the spell more efficient so that it would not require so much power on the part of the magicians who cast it. "I am not done with those adjustments, though."

The current spell worked properly, yes, but Peregrine believed he could do better yet. It would probably take months of revision before he felt satisfied with his work. That did not discourage him, though. What was life for if not for striving to better understand the magical forces flowing through the world?

"I recommend that you avoid mentioned your most recent changes to the spell," Mr. Mattinson advised. "If anyone at Corbin Hall asks you about your work, tell them that the spell hasn't changed since your presentation."

Peregrine's eyes widened. "But that would be a lie!" He had already refined the list of ingredients, and Dora had helped him revise some of the sorcerous components.

"Well, then lie!" Mr. Mattinson sounded irritated now. "You do not want someone else to claim credit for your work, do you?"

"No, I suppose not." Peregrine did not lust for fame or fortune, but he did want his naysayers to know that he, Peregrine Carrington, could accomplish what he set out to do. Besides, he and Dora deserved credit for the many hours they'd put into this work. He could not abide the idea of Blithfield or his friends being lauded for work they hadn't done.

"But I still don't see how anyone could possibly get away with the kind of intellectual theft you are describing," he continued. "Too many people know about my work."

He understood how someone might get away with stealing Mrs. Enfield's ideas, given that she was unlikely to publish or formally present her innovations. But *he* was not an obscure country herbwoman. He was a scholar and an active member of multiple magical organizations. He'd already discussed his meteorite spell with a number of magicians.

Besides, Dora would have known about his work, even if no one else did. Perhaps, he thought uneasily, it was a good thing that Dora was in London, well away from all this. Any danger to him might also be a potential danger to her, since she was his collaborator.

"I thank you for your warning," he said at last. "I believe it would be best if I sent all my notes back to London. If my most recent work is not here, no one can take it from me."

Sending a whole notebook would require considerably more magical energy than sending a single sheet of notepaper, but it was within his power. He still had all the ingredients for the sending spell.

"That might be best." Mr. Mattinson nodded, then cleared his throat. "I don't suppose you would care to have a cup of tea? You must be thirsty after your ride into town."

Peregrine wanted nothing more than to get back to Corbin Hall so he could send his notes to London, but he *was* thirsty. "A cup of tea would be most welcome," he admitted.

The promised cup of tea was accompanied by biscuits, cheese, and conversation. That would have been all very well, except that while the two magicians talked and ate, it began to rain. What started off as a light, refreshing summer rain turned into a torrential downpour by the time Peregrine reached the Green Dragon Inn.

He had intended to retrieve his horse and immediately ride back to Corbin Hall, but by the time he reached the inn, he'd changed his mind. A long ride in this rain would leave him wet to the bone. The road would be filthy with mud, too.

Instead of calling for his horse, Peregrine went into the pub to wait out the downpour. He was not hungry, but he might as well have a pint. He swept his eyes around the half-empty public room, seeing the usual mixture of locals grabbing a pint and travelers taking their rest.

His gaze landed on a slender figure with a mop of dark hair and a cravat rather the worse for his—her?—travels. Peregrine's heart bounded, though he stood as still as if he had seen a ghost. This was no ghost, though: He could tell from the amount of food spread before the traveler. A ghost would not need roast chicken *and* ham *and* a partridge pie. This was Dora: alive, in the flesh, and seemingly quite hungry.

He crossed the room in a few strides. "Mr. Rossini! What are you doing here?" He wished he could greet her with a kiss, but given the way she was dressed, other guests would look askance at that.

Dora gulped down a bite of potatoes and followed it with a swig of wine. "Looking for you, of course. I thought you might appreciate my assistance." She gestured to the empty chair across from her.

Peregrine sat down, feeling no less confused. "Did you come to rescue me, then?" He furrowed his brow doubtfully. Surely he was not in so much danger as *that*?

Instead of answering his question, she pushed the plate of roast chicken towards him. "This isn't as good as what Honora's cook makes, but you might like it."

He wrinkled his nose and shook his head. The chicken looked dry, and who knew how it had been seasoned?

"I'll take my chances on the ham." He was not particularly hungry after all those biscuits, anyway.

Dora nodded, then beckoned to a passing serving maid. "My friend will join me for dinner," she explained. "Please fetch a plate and tableware for him."

Peregrine waited until they were alone to ask, "So why *are* you here, then?"

"I thought you might want my help. Of course you don't need to be *rescued*," she clarified, "since you are a perfectly competent magician. But it sounded like you might be in some sort of trouble."

"I might be," Peregrine agreed. He scanned the room. "We ought not talk about it here." He did not see anyone he recognized, but for all he knew, one of the locals might have connections at Corbin Hall. One never knew when gossip from town might make its way back to Mr. Blithfield.

"Come up to my room after we eat," Dora suggested, "and we can talk there. I want to know *everything* that has happened."

Peregrine took the knife and fork the serving girl handed him and piled ham, peas, and potatoes on his plate. "I don't know that there is much to tell," he admitted. "Just suspicions and rumors." And one missing letter. "It won't be proper for me to be in your bedchamber," he reminded Dora.

Dora snorted. She leaned forward and lowered her voice as she explained, "Everyone here thinks I am a young man. No one will think anything amiss if we hold a private conversation in my room."

He supposed she had a point, but now something even more worrying occurred to him "I appreciate your concern, but was it wise of you to come all this way? When news gets out that you traveled here all by yourself, people will be scandalized." A young lady was never supposed to travel alone. At the very least, she should bring a maid with her. Or did Dora have a lady's maid secretly stashed somewhere? "I assume you *are* alone?"

"Of course I came alone! But we'll think of a good cover story to explain my absence. No one need know that I met you."

Dora did not seem the least bit worried, so Peregrine set aside his concerns and questions. He had a meal to eat, after all.

Wouldn't you know it, though, the ham was dry, and the potatoes were mushy. How could Dora eat such terrible food so voraciously? This was precisely why he hated dining at unfamiliar inns! He confined himself to peas and a dinner roll, which was at least freshly baked. He likewise limited himself to trivial conversation, though he had so many important things he wanted to tell Dora.

After dinner, he followed her up two flights of stairs to a small but comfortable room. The chamber contained a washstand with ewer and washbasin, a single wooden chair, a small wardrobe, and a moderately large bed.

While Dora shut the door and turned the key in the lock, Peregrine took a seat at the edge of the bed. He intended to leave the chair for Dora. But, to his surprise, she sat down next to him, affectionately bumping her shoulder against his.

"You know, I don't really like your traveling without me," she said conversationally. "I missed you."

He turned his head toward her and opened his mouth to reassure her that he had missed her, too. But when their eyes met, all the words ran out of his head like water from a leaky cistern.

It was not so much that he kissed her or that she kissed him as that they were both hungrily kissing each other. Peregrine ran a hand through Dora's hair. The familiar texture of her loose curls was both comforting and arousing.

Dora cupped his face with one hand as she teased at his lower lip. When she kissed the underside of the jaw, a tingle traveled all the way down to his toes, making his groin tighten along the way.

"Don't," he rasped.

"Oh, you don't like that? I'm sorry." She drew back immediately.

"No, I *do* like it." He leaned back, took a deep breath, and tried to collect his scattered wits. The two of them ought not be embracing like this on a bed, especially in a room with a locked door.

"I liked it too much," he explained. "That was—This is—I think we probably ought to sit on opposite sides of the room or something." Maybe he should move to that empty chair before they got further carried away.

"What? Why?" Dora wrinkled her forehead.

Feeling equal parts embarrassment and arousal, Peregrine averted his eyes. "I'm afraid we might end up doing something we would regret." Or at least, something they *ought* to regret. Or something other people would *think* they ought to regret. Something—

Dora interrupted his tangled cognitions. "Are you sure you would regret it? Because I wouldn't."

CHAPTER SEVENTEEN

Dora saw from Peregrine's widening eyes that she'd shocked him. The gold flecks in his irises looking brighter than usual in contrast to the enlarged pupils.

"Perhaps we aren't talking about the same thing?" he suggested.

"I am talking about going to bed with you," Dora explained. "What were *you* talking about?"

It certainly sounded like a good idea to her. She felt flushed from her head to her feet, and her whole body thirsted for more. She hadn't wanted to stop kissing her lover. She hadn't wanted to let him go. She felt disappointed to be sitting a foot away from him now.

Peregrine cleared his throat. "Er, the same thing, I suppose. I mean, I was thinking about going to bed with you. But, you know, people would think—"

She did not let him finish his sentence. "I don't care what people think. We are going to get married anyway, aren't we? So, what does it matter?"

Neither she nor Peregrine were particularly religious, and she found the arguments in favor of premarital chastity unconvincing at best. Most bachelors of the *ton* seemed to keep mistresses, take lovers, or visit brothels, and it did not seem fair that young ladies were not allowed to do the same.

"I don't have a contraception charm with me," Peregrine

pointed out. "If I lie with you, I might get you with child."

"Oh." Dora sighed. That was a good objection. "I do not want to fall pregnant. Not yet." If ever. Neither she nor Peregrine had any need of an heir. She supposed she might want a child someday, if only to see what happened when the Carrington and Grantly bloodlines mingled. Combine the Carrington eccentricity with the Grantly impulsiveness, and who knew what a child of theirs might do?

But Dora did not want to fall pregnant now, when there was still so much of the world to explore. She'd only left home a few months ago, and she had only sampled a little of one London Season. There were many things she wanted to do before exploring parenthood, *if* she ever did choose that.

"Of course, there are other things we could do instead." Peregrine suggested this straightforwardly, not putting a seductive or salacious emphasis on any of the words. He waited patiently for her response.

Dora swallowed, and her heart began to pound more heavily again. She thought she had some idea of what he meant. Thanks to Honora's talks with her, Dora probably knew more about bedroom activities than most unmarried young ladies. She knew there were different ways people could please each other in bed, apart from traditional sexual relations.

"I'm game," she said.

A smile lit up her beloved's face. "First, let me take off that cravat you're wearing. It's crooked, and that's been irritating me since the moment I saw you in the dining room."

Dora laughed out loud. Some of the laughter might have stemmed from nervousness, but most of it came from genuine amusement. Of all the things Peregrine could do now that they were alone, he wanted to start by untying her cravat!

But her laughter faded as he leaned forward and slowly loosened the knotted neckcloth. She would not have believed it if anyone had told her that so domestic a task could be seductive. Gentlemen had help with their cravats all the time, didn't they? It was perfectly normal for a valet to help his employer dress and undress. And, for that matter, Peregrine himself was the one who usually tied her cravat, since she had still not mastered the art. There had never been anything the least bit erotic about him helping her tie it properly.

But, she discovered, Peregrine *untying* her cravat was an entirely different story—at least when they sat alone on a bed, heat filling the eyes so intently fixed on her. She swallowed nervously. What was she supposed to do? Should she untie *his* cravat?

Before she could figure out how to respond, he had finished. He dropped the crumpled muslin onto the floor. Then he brushed his lips against the newly exposed skin of her throat. Dora sucked in her breath.

Peregrine drew back. "Oh, did that bother you? I am sorry!"

For some reason, it was more difficult to form words than usual. "No. It did not bother me. Um, should I untie your cravat for you?"

He shook his head. "Let me do that myself, since the knot can be tricky. But you can unbutton my waistcoat if you like."

Dora liked that very much. By now she was quite familiar with the process of buttoning and unbuttoning her own waist-coat, but again, she found it quite different to undress someone else. She worried she would fumble or tear a button out in her haste, but no matter how heavily her heart pounded, her hands continued to move slowly and steadily, as if there were no haste at all. As if she undressed handsome young gentlemen every day.

They stripped each other slowly, dropping their discarded garments on the floor. She had seen Peregrine in his shirtsleeves before, but not in any further state of undress. It was fascinating to watch him shed layer after layer—topcoat, waistcoat, shirt, pantaloons—until he was clad in nothing at all.

Dimly, Dora wondered if it bothered him that he was not neatly folding his clothes and putting them in their proper place. Normally, he put his things away on shelves, drawers, or in baskets rather than leaving them scattered about the room. His carelessness said a good deal about how focused he was on their activity.

Silently, he pulled off Dora's shirt, which was rather worse for the wear, as she had been too hungry to change her travel-worn clothes yet. She had washed up a little, but. . .

"I am probably filthy from two days on the road," she blurted out. She ought to have thought of that earlier. She could have called for a bath if she had known anyone would see her naked. But how could she have known that? She had not expected to see Peregrine until tomorrow.

That did not faze him. "You have a wash basin." He nodded in the direction of the washstand. "Would you like me to help you wash?" Somehow, he made this sound like a perfectly reasonable proposal rather than a scandalous proposition.

Nevertheless, his suggestion turned her into a babbling fool. "Um. Yes. I did bring my own soap." She liked the scented soap used in the Valance household so much that she hadn't wanted to go without it while away.

If the prospect of being washed by her lover seemed titillating, her expectations quickly received a dash of cold water—or rather, room temperature water, because she had not thought to ring for hot water. Though it felt good to get thoroughly clean, she did not feel at all disposed to linger over the task of washing. As it was, the process dampened her ardor a little.

But Peregrine brought the flush back to her skin very quickly, by tracing circles around one of her nipples—first with a finger, then with his tongue.

"That feels good," Dora told him. Then she fell silent, wanting to devote her whole attention to the sensations his touch created. She liked the way he cupped one hand behind her backside as he continued to tease her breasts.

But when she tried running a hand down his back, admiring the length of his long, lightly muscled torso, he shivered.

"Don't, please. I don't like to be stroked like that."

That surprised her. *She* certainly liked feeling his hands on her body. But Peregrine was different from her in so many ways.

"What do you like, then?" Her voice sounded uncertain even to her own ears. She was treading very new ground here.

He smiled at her. "I like getting to see you—all of you—and getting to touch you. When you are satisfied, I can show you how to pleasure me. But right now, I want to please you."

As he spoke, he slowly moved his hand down to the warm, aching place between her legs. He rested it there, leaving her agonizingly close to satisfaction.

"I am not used to satisfying a woman," he admitted. "What can I do please you?"

"Move your hand in circles," she suggested. "Light circles." She lay back on the bed to give him better access. Then she touched the sensitive nub between her folds. "Right around here."

"Like this?" He moved his hand in a slow, tight circle around her sweet spot, fanning the flame of her arousal.

"Oh, yes, that's good," she gasped. After that, she communicated mostly through sharp intakes of breath and sighs, followed by a long, drawn-out "Oh!" when the mounting tension finally broke. Every other sensation fell away and she was aware only of the circling motion of Peregrine's hand, her spasming pelvic muscles, and the powerful release.

When the peak ended, she lay with her eyes still closed as she tried to remember how to breathe normally. She had experienced such physical transports when alone, but emotionally, it felt quite different to do so in response to someone else's touch. She needed a moment to collect herself.

"All right?" he asked. "Are you satisfied?"

Dora opened her eyes and smiled shakily. "Um. Yes." For now, at least. She rolled toward Peregrine so she could kiss him on the cheek. "Thank you."

"You are very welcome." He cupped her face with one long-fingered hand and kissed her back.

"What should I do for you, then?" Dora watched as the corners of her lover's mouth turned up in a slight smile. But he hesitated to speak. "You promised to tell me what to do," she reminded him.

"I know." He gently ruffled her hair. "I am just trying to figure out what would be best. I am not used to pulling out, so I don't think I ought to try to tup you. I might not be able to control myself. Especially since it has been so long."

So long since what? Dora decided not to ask. She knew Peregrine had bedded other women before, but now did not seem like the right time to ask him about his experiences. His past did not particularly worry her; she felt confident there would be no other women in the future.

"What should we do, then?" she prompted.

"I think it would be simplest if you just used your hand on me," he replied. "I will show you."

He rifled through the pile of discarded clothing on the floor until he found a handkerchief. Then he guided her hand to his stiff member and let her explore it. She had never seen an aroused man before and found his erection fascinating. Didn't it hurt for something to swell that much? She could not imagine how it could be comfortable.

But when she ran her hand up and down its length, he sighed in pleasure. "That's good, but wrap your hand around it—a little firmer than that, please. And a little slower."

Dora watched his face as she slid her hand up and down, trying to gauge from his expression what felt better. The sudden contortion of his face startled her, but it took only a second for her to realize that it meant that he was spilling himself into the handkerchief. She glanced down, curious about the process.

"This is all very messy," she observed. Who in the world would have imagined that this was how humans reproduced, how they expressed love, how they sought pleasure? Bodies were such funny things!

"Yes, unfortunately." He wrinkled his nose.

Dora dug about for the washcloth they had used earlier, and she took a turn washing him. Then she lay down next to him, leaving a little space between their bodies in case he did not want contact. Peregrine did not always like being touched. But he rolled towards her, draped one arm around her, and leaned his head against hers.

"This is pleasant," he murmured. "I have missed you so much, you know. I wish your bloody uncle would give his permission for us to get married."

Dora did not want to think about any of her relatives just now (not even the ones she liked), but his words reminded her of the plan she'd concocted on her road to Carlisle. She eyed her betrothed thoughtfully and decided that the moment might be propitious for her suggestion.

She cleared her throat first. "I've been thinking. Since we are so close to Scotland, why don't we run up to Gretna Green and get married? We may never have a better opportunity."

CHAPTER EIGHTEEN

PEREGRINE BLINKED AS he absorbed Dora's suggestion. It was the obvious solution to their legal battles, but he saw what he feared might be an insurmountable obstacle.

"I don't think I can do that. I promised Roderick I wouldn't elope with you, remember?"

Roderick had read Peregrine a thorough lecture on the subject the day after the meteor shower. Even at the time, Peregrine could not help wondering what it would have been like to have an older brother who felt just a *little* less responsibility toward his extended family. But Roderick was Roderick, and it was no use wishing otherwise. If Peregrine and Dora married each other across the anvil, Roderick would certainly have something to say about the matter.

"Roderick thought eloping would damage your reputation too much," Peregrine continued. "And my reputation too, for that matter. Some people already think the Carringtons are not good *ton*."

He pulled a face, thinking of the times Abigail had gotten the cut direct from high sticklers who refused to accept either her radical political views or her decision to live without the chaperonage of an older relative. It had been worse when Valance lived at Carrington House, because many people assumed Valance and Abigail were lovers. Even now, there were plenty of people who were suspicious of a spinster who lived with only a companion and a younger brother to lend her countenance.

Dora snorted. "As if I cared about that! I only cared so much about my reputation because I wanted to convince Uncle Robert I was responsible enough to get married. But if we got married in Scotland, I wouldn't have to worry about Uncle Robert anymore. Married women don't need guardians."

Probably, Peregrine thought, because it was assumed that a married woman's husband functioned as a guardian. His frown curved up into a slight smile, because it was absurd to think he could or should exert such authority over Dora.

Dora poked him in the arm. "What are you smirking about?"

"Oh, I was just thinking about how ridiculous the law of coverture is," he explained. "As if I knew how to manage your life better than you did!"

"As if you had time to spare from your work to manage any-one else's life!" Dora scoffed.

Peregrine nodded. That was a good point, too. Managing his own affairs was taxing enough; he did not want to be responsible for another perfectly competent adult.

He knew, though, that many women found coverture a bur-den rather than a joke. Abigail and Susan's volunteer work brought them into frequent contact with women who had suffered under England's matrimonial laws, and he'd heard some of their stories.

His smile faded as he recalled women whose husbands stole their hard-earned wages for beer or gaming; women who had no say in family decisions; women who suffered physical abuse for which there was no legal recourse, because the law allowed a man to discipline his wife.

The laws that allowed men so much authority over their wives had never made much sense to Peregrine. Anyone who actually *knew* a woman must realize that women were quite as capable as men. Did lawmakers never bother to listen to the women in their lives?

Peregrine caught and held Dora's gaze. "I hope you know I

would never try to control you, even if I could." No matter what the law allowed, he had no desire to be a domestic dictator.

Dora brushed a strand of hair away from his eyes. "I know that! But back to my question. . . will you go to Scotland with me? We would never have a better opportunity. The border's only a few miles away, isn't it? We could leave in the morning, get married, and be back here before dinner time."

He frowned. She had a point, but. . . "I *promised*," he repeated.

"Is it really so terrible if you break your promise?"

Dora's beseeching gaze cut him to the heart. It hurt to even draw a breath. Was there any way he could justify breaking his promise to Roderick? He tried to think of a loophole, but he couldn't see any way around his promise. As for simply breaking his word—the very thought made him sick. What good was a promise if it could be so easily discarded?

Peregrine reluctantly shook his head. "I really am sorry, but I cannot go against my word like that."

Dora studied him for a long, anxious moment. Finally, she nodded. "I understand. I cannot ask you to do anything that would violate your conscience. You should forget I ever mentioned it." She turned her face away from him. "I think I would like to rest now, if you don't mind."

Her abrupt dismissal felt like a slap in the face. Dora was often blunt, but she had never shut him out like this. He wanted to speak a comforting word, but had no idea what to say. "Of course. I suppose I'd better go back to Corbin Hall, then?"

"Tonight?" She whipped her head around to stare at him. "But it's pitch black out there! And what about the rain?"

"Oh, right, the rain." More interesting events had driven the rainstorm entirely out of Peregrine's mind. But Dora was right. Even if the rain had stopped, the night probably would be too dark for him to ride along unfamiliar roads. "Tomorrow morning, then." Blithfield and the other guests might worry about Peregrine's extended absence, but he could see no help for that.

"Tomorrow," Dora repeated. "Very well. But I really have had a long day, and I ought to rest." She turned away from him again, plumped up her pillow, and lay down. Then she pulled the blanket more tightly around herself.

Peregrine eyed her blanket-shrouded form, feeling deeply unsettled. Dora seemed to understand his objection to eloping, and he thought she had accepted his decision. But a breach now gaped between them, and he had no idea how to bridge it. He lay down and stared up at the ceiling, wondering what he could have done differently.

HE MUST HAVE slept, because the next time he opened his eyes, the rainy twilight outside had turned to full night. Next to him, Dora tossed and turned. He could have ignored that, until he heard her sniffling. *Was she crying?*

"Is something wrong?" he whispered.

"Oh, no. Just having trouble sleeping. This isn't a particularly comfortable mattress."

She was right about the mattress, but her voice sounded shaky and strained. Yes, Peregrine concluded, she had been crying. His own throat tightened in response.

"You are unhappy because I don't want to elope with you?" he guessed.

She did not deny it. She merely said, "It is foolish of me, I know. It's not as if we *need* to get married immediately."

Was it foolish, though? Dora had taken an enormous risk to see Peregrine. By now she was very good at playing the part of a young man, but there was no guarantee that she could make it all the way back to London without being caught. She would be absolutely ruined if anyone knew she'd shared a bed with him tonight.

If they married tomorrow, people would undoubtedly gossip about the elopement, just as Roderick had feared. The people who already looked askance at the Carrington family would be even more likely to shun them. But there would be an even bigger scandal if Dora returned home unmarried and ruined.

Roderick wouldn't want that, would he? Peregrine himself did not want such a scandal. While marrying across the anvil was not at all proper, it would at the very least make it clear that Peregrine's attentions were honorable.

"I wish I hadn't made that promise to Roderick," he grumbled. His older brother ought to have known better than to ask for such a promise, and Peregrine ought to have known better than to give it.

Dora sat up, her eyes widening. "But Peregrine, you didn't elope with me. I ran away on my own. You had nothing to do with that. Roderick cannot blame you for it."

"I suppose that's true." The elopement had been all Dora's idea. In fact, if Peregrine had known she intended to come to his rescue, he would have discouraged her. There was always some danger involved in long-distance travel, especially on the public stage.

Peregrine sat up, propping a pillow behind his back. He played idly with the edge of the blanket as he worked through all the implications. He desperately wanted a way to make things right with Dora while satisfying his sense of honor. Until now, he hadn't believed that was possible.

"Do you really think I wouldn't be breaking my promise to Roderick if we married in Scotland?" he asked cautiously.

Dora gnawed on her lower lip. "I suppose it depends. Did you promise not to *marry me* in Scotland, or not to *elope* to Scotland? What was the exact wording?"

"A good question." Peregrine always liked to be precise in his wording. He gazed off into space as he reviewed his memory. "He asked me not 'run off to Scotland' with you. I promised not to elope. We never discussed the possibility of your traveling north on your own." Neither he nor his brother would have ever imagined this particular situation.

"Exactly." She sounded smug. "And you kept your word, Peregrine. You didn't 'run off' with me. I ran off by myself. If you married me, you might be breaking the spirit of the promise, but not the promise itself. At least, that's how I see it." She glanced at him out of the corner of her eye and smiled crookedly.

Peregrine needed no more convincing. "Very well. Let's do it. Let's get married." When his eyes met hers, his heart performed some complicated gymnastics.

"Really?" She sounded almost breathless.

"Really," he assured her. "Tomorrow, if you like. I could write a note to Mr. Blithfield to say that I've been called away by urgent family matters, and that I will return in a few days to get my things. And then we will go get married."

When her smile reached the dimples in her cheeks, he knew he'd said the right thing.

"I would like that." Her eyes softened as she looked at him. "I know you do not like doing things spur-of-the-moment, so this probably seemed like an unreasonable request. Thank you for indulging me."

"It is not unreasonable for me to put your happiness before anything else," he said earnestly. "Because you are the brightest, truest star in my sky."

That must have been the right thing to say, too, because she leaned in to give him a long, lingering kiss. He kissed her back, and what with one thing leading to another, he ended up being very glad that he stayed at the inn rather than riding back to Corbin Hall that night.

THE NEXT MORNING, Peregrine wrote a note for Mr. Blithfield, full of apologies and half truths (Dora helped him invent excuses). He sent the note and his borrowed horse back to Corbin Hall in the care of a stable boy eager to earn a few coins for his labor.

While Peregrine arranged for the hire of a post chaise, Dora snuck into an unoccupied storage room and transformed herself. She had fortuitously packed a set of her women's clothing just in case. Clad in a pretty green walking dress, with a demure bonnet covering her dark curls, she looked, spoke, and walked like a genteel young lady who would never dream of traveling incognito.

If anyone had looked carefully at Dora, they might have noticed her resemblance to the dark-haired young man who'd just checked out of the inn, but no one took a second look at her. And if anyone thought it was odd that Peregrine, who had shown up at the inn by himself, left in the company of a fashionably dressed young lady, they kept such thoughts to themselves.

Last night's rain left the roads muddy, but at least the sun shone brightly today. The postilion whistled as the horses trotted up the highway towards Scotland.

"If this were a proper elopement, someone would be chasing us on horseback, trying to prevent the wedding." Dora glanced out the window, her wistful expression suggesting that the lack of pursuit disappointed her.

"The only people who would try to prevent us from marrying are your uncle and your stepmother," Peregrine pointed out. *His* family had no objection to the match. Apart from Roderick, most of them would not even shake their heads at the hasty wedding, since they knew how obstinate the Grantlys were being.

Dora protested. "Lady Grantly is not really my stepmother! She is only my father's wife. That does not make her my relation."

Peregrine opened his mouth to point out that that was, in fact, the definition of *stepmother*, but Dora glared at him so fiercely that he closed it again.

"They will not have any control over me after this." Dora leaned back against the carriage squabs, looking relieved, if not downright smug.

"But if your uncle is your trustee, he can keep you from accessing your fortune," Peregrine reminded her.

The scowl momentarily returned to her face. "Uncle Robert can keep that money for all I care. We do not need it."

That was certainly true, thanks to the generosity of Great-Uncle Perry's will, but if they ever had children, they might want that money. Still, Peregrine decided not to quibble. Instead, he changed the subject by asking where they ought to live in London.

Dora had no objection to living at Carrington House. The problem was how to make room for another person in a fairly crowded townhouse. They spent the remainder of the journey trying to work out what things could be moved to the attic or disposed of in order to clear out the guest room next to Peregrine's bedchamber. It would, he supposed, be a lot of fuss and pother. But it would be worth it to have Dora living with him permanently.

Dora and Peregrine were still debating how best to use the breakfast room, which had once been Valance's workroom, when the chaise rolled to a stop. Peregrine's heart bounded at the sight of the blacksmith shop. They had arrived, and his life was about to change forever.

CHAPTER NINETEEN

T HE BLACKSMITH STOOD in the doorway, studying the newly arrived couple with narrowed eyes. "Can you I help you, sir?" he asked Peregrine.

"We wish to be married over the anvil." Peregrine spoke briskly and matter-of-factly. "Can you do that?"

The man nodded, as if he had already guessed their errand. He probably had. Why else would a well-dressed young couple get out of a traveling chaise in front of his shop?

"Aye. Step into my smithy, and I'll fetch some witnesses." He gestured toward the entryway.

While Peregrine paid and dismissed the postilion, Dora wandered into the smithy and looked about the room. The anvil stood atop a solid stone in the middle of the room. The room had no ceiling, merely the open, soot-stained timbers of the roof. At one point in time, it must have been an active smithy, but there was no sign of recent labor.

The blacksmith returned quickly, with a pair of elderly men in tow. The two men stood near the wall and chatted softly to themselves while the smith fetched a hammer and his register. He placed the large book on the anvil and turned to a page in the middle.

"May I have your names and residences, please?" he asked.

"I am Mr. Peregrine Carrington, of London, and of Carrington Abbey, in Surrey."

"And I am Miss Dora Rossini, of London." She hesitated a moment before adding "And Grantly Manor, in Kent." Grantly Manor no longer seemed like home to her, but she had lived there most of her life. It probably ought to be recorded as such.

Brides and grooms were rumored to look nervous during their weddings, but Peregrine did not display any signs of anxiety. He stood straight and tall, and spoke as calmly and confidently as ever.

Dora did not feel nervous, either. Not exactly. But she felt giddy and jittery, as if she'd drunk an entire pot of coffee. She found it hard to stand still and keep quiet, when she wanted to skip about the room.

"And you come here of your free will?" The blacksmith scrutinized both of them, but Dora thought his gaze lingered longest on her, as if he thought she might have been coerced into the marriage.

"Yes," they said at nearly the same time.

Dora met Peregrine's eyes and smiled. If there had been any coercion involved, she would have been the one responsible: Peregrine would never have pressured her to marry him against her own wishes.

Peregrine's mouth did not move, but his eyes crinkled in response. Maybe he was thinking the same thing.

"Very well, then." The blacksmith nodded and shifted position to face Peregrine. "Do you take this woman to be your lawful wedded wife, and forsaking all others, keep to her as long as you both shall live?"

"I do."

Then the blacksmith looked at Dora as he repeated the question.

"I do." She was surprised at how calm and steady her voice sounded. She wanted to sing or shout or run down the street and tell every stranger she saw that she was getting married. "And now the ring, if you please?" He looked at Peregrine and Dora as if he expected them to produce a wedding ring out of thin air.

Dora's mouth fell ajar. She did not wear a ring. She had not brought one with her because she had not expected to elope. She looked at Peregrine and raised her brows, asking a silent question.

Peregrine frowned and shook his head. "I am afraid we haven't got a ring. Does that mean we can't be married?"

"No, I can make up for the lack." The smith walked over to a worktable along one wall and rustled through a box. "My apprentice likes to make rings out of horseshoe nails. You can use this."

Dora reached out her hand, and he dropped the ring into her palm. It was nothing but a nail that had been bent in a circle, then polished until it shone. She pulled the glove off her left hand so Peregrine could place the ring on her finger as he said the traditional words of betrothal.

"Now you must hold hands." The smith waited until they had done so before saying, "Repeat after me: 'What God has joined let no man put asunder.'"

She repeated the words, clinging tightly to Peregrine's hand. Her voice sounded distant and unfamiliar, as if some stranger spoke on her behalf. Perhaps she was a little nervous after all. When Peregrine squeezed her hand reassuringly, she looked up at him, intending to smile. But all she could do was stare at him, transfixed by the strangeness of the moment. The blacksmith was saying something in a loud, clear voice, but she could not make out a single word. She had eyes and ears only for her love.

When the blacksmith brought his hammer down, making the anvil ring, she jumped.

"Congratulations!" one of the witnesses called.

"That's it?" Dora could hardly believe it. The whole ceremony had taken no more than five minutes.

"That's it," the blacksmith confirmed. "Except you must sign the register." He had pen and ink ready for them. He must have performed many weddings. He seemed to have the entire procedure down pat.

Peregrine signed in a neat, tidy signature. The elation fizzing through Dora's veins made it hard to write steadily, so she signed her maiden name in a sloppy swoop that wavered across the page. And that was it. Peregrine handed the blacksmith a few bright sovereigns. Then he picked up their valises, and he and Dora walked out into the bright June morning.

Dora blinked her eyes against the bright sunlight, then looked around. How strange that the world looked exactly as it had ten minutes ago. To her, everything had changed in the blink of the eye. She had become someone else: Dora Carrington. Or had she? She thought about the disguises she had worn in the last few months and decided that she remained the same person no matter what she called herself.

"I suppose," Peregrine said, "we ought to see if the inn has room for us. And then I will find the nearest apothecary shop."

"Apothecary shop? Are you unwell?" Dora studied him, puzzled. She didn't see any signs of illness. On the contrary, he smiled at her question.

"No, but I don't have the ingredients to work a contraception charm myself, so I will have to buy one."

"Oh, of course!" She clamped down on the sudden burst of amusement she felt. There were a few people out in the street already watching the newlyweds with interest. She did not want to draw further attention by raucous laughter. Or any other kind of laughter, for that matter.

Besides, there really was nothing funny about what Peregrine had said. If she did not want to become pregnant, they would need such a charm. She could not work medical magic herself. And she certainly *did* want to experiment further with Peregrine in bed.

"I could do with a cup of tea," she announced. Maybe that would settle her unruly nerves. "Let's see if the innkeeper can serve us a bit of luncheon."

When they reached the inn, the innkeeper announced what he thought would be bad news: "I'm afraid I've only one room left for tonight. There's a badger-baiting match nearby, and a lot of rowdy young men from out of town have already bespoken rooms." His scrunched-up face suggested he disapproved of badger-baiting, the rowdy young men, or both.

"Only one room?" Dora said gravely. "That *is* a problem." Then she shamed herself by bursting out in an undignified chortle. Of course, there *would* be only room. God forbid that there should ever be an inn that had separate rooms for a pair of attractive young people traveling together!

The innkeeper and her husband both stared at her. Peregrine's eyes merely widened slightly, but the innkeeper gaped outright.

"Are you quite all right?" Peregrine asked. "I hope you are not sickening with something."

He had not seen the joke, she supposed. She cleared her throat and did her best to repress her amusement. "Just a bit of dust in my throat. I shall be right as a trivet as soon as I have a cup of tea." She turned to the innkeeper and gave him her most reassuring smile. "One room will do quite well for us, thank you." What with them being married and all.

"If you'll just step this way, ma'am, I can get you that cup of tea," he offered.

The cup of tea did settle her nerves, as did the salad and cold meat that the inn offered for lunch. So did the long, warm bath she had after the meal. It felt good to wash nearly three days of travel away. And then, though it seemed rather anticlimactic after the events of the morning, Dora took an afternoon nap. She did not normally sleep in the day, but she had a few nights' sleep to make up.

She expected to nap lightly, for no more than half an hour. Instead, she slept for hours. Peregrine shook her awake when it was time for dinner. The cook at this inn, unfortunately, did not seem as talented as the one in the Carlisle. Or maybe, Dora thought charitably, whoever made the meal was having an off day. At least the inn had been able to seat them in a private dining room, rather than in the public one.

"Did you find an apothecary shop?" she asked as she contemplated the cheese and biscuits that had been brought out as a dessert course. The biscuits looked hard and unappetizing, and the cheese could best be described as *dubious*.

"Oh, yes. I wasn't particular impressed with the apothecary, but this was made by a local midwife, and it seems to be a well-worked charm." He reached into his pocket and pulled out a circlet made of multicolored silken threads braided together.

"Thread magic?" Dora touched it lightly with one finger.

Though her sister saw magic as lights and colors, Dora perceived it as sound and sensation. To her, the bracelet hummed with power. She frowned, because it occurred to her that what she experienced as a pleasant, musical hum might very well strike Peregrine as a discord.

"Must you be the one to wear that? Won't it bother you?" He was far more sensitive to magic than she was.

He shook his head. "This type of charm can be worn by either a man or a woman. It's so well-made that it might not irritate me, but—"

"I will wear it," Dora said promptly. She took the bracelet from him and slid it onto her wrist. He was right about it being well-made. She could only feel the presence of the magic when she looked for it. Otherwise, it faded into the background. "It must be difficult to work medical magic that is both effective and unobtrusive."

Most people could not sense magic at all, but for those who could, wearing a charm like this might be rather awkward. She doubted that anyone enjoyed being distracted from bedsport by a spell that advertised its power too loudly.

Peregrine shrugged. "That is why it is best to get these charms from an expert. Most general healers would not be able to make something that was both effective and unobtrusive." He frowned. "I knew a chap at Oxford who could not stand any sort of charm on his person at all. I think he had to use a normal condom when he visited a School of Venus. But of course, those are not nearly as reliable at preventing infection as the ones that are reinforced by magic—"

Dora interrupted him with a question. "School of Venus? Do you mean a house of ill fame?" She had never heard it called that. But then, few gentlemen were willing to discuss the subject in her presence. If Sir Isaac had ever visited such establishments, he had certainly never mentioned it to his children.

"Oh, yes, I suppose that's a more polite term for it," he agreed. "*Academy* is the most common term I know, but I never much liked that word. Unless one has some context, it might be unclear whether it meant a brothel or an actual educational institute."

"How often do you talk to other people about brothels?" Dora asked, fascinated.

"Oh, not that often. I mean, I didn't *talk* about them nearly as often as I used to visit them," he explained. "What?"

She had broken into laughter again. Probably a good thing, because otherwise, she might have blurted out an intrusive question. She really didn't need to know how often Peregrine had visited brothels in the past.

He smiled ruefully. "I suppose most gentlemen would not talk about this with a genteel lady even if they were married to her."

"Probably not," Dora agreed, sobering a little. "But you can talk to me about anything, you know."

He dropped his gaze to stare down at his half empty plate. "It is kind of you to say that. But you don't really mean it, do you? No one wants to hear *everything* I think." He spoke with a certainty probably born of experience.

Painful experience, Dora guessed. She bit her lip as she chose her words. "I don't need an endless monologue of all the thoughts running in your brain," she admitted.

Privately, she doubted she could keep up with that. Having no false modesty, she knew that her own mind worked swiftly, but she also knew that it did not work quite the same way as

Peregrine's. That wasn't just her imagination, either; Valance had also mentioned that Peregrine's thoughts sometimes flowed in different channels rather than following the usual course.

"But," she continued, "you should be able to say anything you like to me, even if it's something forbidden by proper etiquette. You are my husband, after all."

A smile split his face. "In that case, you should know that right now, all I can think about is taking you to bed."

CHAPTER TWENTY

I NSTEAD OF BLUSHING like a stereotypical bashful bride, Dora chuckled, crinkling her eyes and displaying the dimples in her cheeks. Peregrine's heart performed another one of those summersaults that only Dora elicited.

"What else *would* you be thinking of on your wedding night?" she replied. "I am done eating. Would you like to go to bed now?"

"Yes." He put down his fork immediately. He had not eaten much, but then, it had not been a particularly good dinner. He would far rather have Dora.

Before he could offer her his arm to escort her upstairs, she took hold of his hand, intertwining her fingers with his. As they walked up the staircase, he glanced about sheepishly, not liking the idea of other people watching them. Gretna Green was so well known for its hasty weddings that other guests at the inn might very guess that they were newlyweds. He did not want to draw unwelcome attention.

But Dora squeezed his hand reassuringly, as if she had somehow guessed what he was thinking, and he relaxed. In any case, no one passed them either on the stairs or in the corridor. Then they were in their own chamber. As soon as Dora turned the key in the lock, he took her in his arms and kissed her.

He had meant to be deliberate and gentle and slow, knowing that all of this was still very new to her, but his kiss turned desperate quickly. When her tongue swept lightly along his lips, a shiver that was half shock and half desire swept the whole length of his body, ending with his groin.

"I like that," he gasped, "but just so you know, I don't like having someone else's tongue in my mouth."

For the first time, it occurred to him that perhaps they should have talked about these things *before* they said their vows. His "delicate nerves"—or whatever made him different from other people—affected what he liked in bed, just as they affected how he ate, traveled, and interacted with people. His love for Dora was as strong and certain as gravity itself, but there were some things abouts him that even the deepest, truest love could not change.

"I am sorry if that disappoints you," he continued, though his tightening throat made it hard to speak. "I—"

"I will only be disappointed if you stand there apologizing when I want to feel your mouth against mine!" she said fiercely.

"To hear is to obey." He pulled her closer and put his words into action.

Together, they stumbled toward the bed. He briefly wondered if he ought to remove his clothes himself to make sure that they would not get wrinkled or crushed again. Then he quit worrying about it and devoted all of his attention to Dora.

Last night, they had undressed each other slowly, almost reverently. Today, they were both eager to feel skin touching skin again. This time, he let her untie his neckcloth, though her untrained fingers fumbled with the knot.

For a fleeting moment, Peregrine thought of the skilled professionals who had been his lovers in the past. Then he firmly closed the door on that thought. There could be no comparison between those women and Dora. His previous sexual encounters had all been a matter of receiving services in exchange for a fee. Though he'd preferred some women of pleasure over others, they had been favorites merely because they had been good at remembering what he did and did not like. He had seen only brief glimpses of the personalities that lay beneath their professional veneer, and he had revealed little about himself beyond his preferences in bed.

Dora was different, because he loved her. All of her, not merely her enticing body. She was intelligent and forthright and bold and—great starry heavens, that felt *good*. He gasped as she ran her hand up and down his erection. How had she gotten so good at this in the span of a single day?

"If you keep doing that," he warned, "this is going to end much sooner than I want."

She took her hand away, but made up for the lack by pressing her body against his. By now she wore only a plain white shift.

"What would you like to do, then?"

"Um." He gulped, unsure how to put his desires into appropriate words.

She must have guessed why he hesitated, because she reminded him, "I told you that you could say whatever you want to me."

He took her at her word and blurted it out. "I want to tear your shift off, tumble into bed with you, bury myself in your sweet, soft heat, and rut. And I want to do that *now*."

Her eyes widened and her mouth fell ajar.

Peregrine's face flushed. "You asked!" he reminded her.

The corners of Dora's mouth tipped up. "I asked," she agreed. "Let's do that, then."

His heart lurched in his chest. "I love you so very much." He could not remember whether he'd said that before, but it seemed important that she hear it now.

Dora's eyes seemed to brighten, though of course that was not literally possible. But something about her entire face changed as she replied, "I love you too." Then she stood on her toes to press a soft kiss against his lips.

They tumbled into bed. Dora shoved the heavy blanket out of the way. He pressed his face against her chest, dropping kisses against her delicately sculpted breasts. He sighed as he caught a whiff of the floral soap she used. Already, that scent had become dear to him.

"I hope you know you can never stop using that brand of soap," he warned her. "Nothing else would smell right."

"It's the same with you and that clove scented soap you use. It's—" She abandoned whatever she meant to say the moment he began teasing her nipple with his tongue.

He loved every inch of her body, but if he was honest, he loved some inches more than others. This part was definitely in the top five. Maybe the top three, but he could only determine that after further investigation.

Peregrine reached down to stroke her vulva, trying to remember Dora's instructions from last night. When she moaned softy, his aroused member twitched in response.

"Now?" he whispered hopefully. He could be very articulate under some circumstances, but not in this particular situation. With other parts of his body demanding so much of Peregrine's attention, it was all he could do to remember how to communicate at all.

"Yes," she breathed.

He covered her with his body. She wrapped her arms around him and opened her legs to welcome him. Peregrine sighed contentedly as he sank into her warmth, but Dora gasped.

He opened his eyes. "I'm sorry, did that hurt?"

She bit her lip and nodded. "A little. It isn't too bad."

"I am so very sorry." He withdrew and rolled away, coming to rest by her side "Was I too rough?"

Dora shook her head. "Isn't it normal for it to hurt a little the first time? I am sure it will get better later." She licked her lips, suggesting she might not be as confident as she wanted him to think.

"I suppose you are right." How had he forgotten that? He ought to have been more considerate. "Do you want us to rest try again later?"

"I will be all right," she insisted. "You don't have to stop. *You* are enjoying this, aren't you?"

"I don't think I can enjoy it if you are uncomfortable." Perhaps that was a drawback of having a *lover*, in every sense of the word, rather than a mere bedmate. Dora's experience was as important as his own. Maybe more important. Peregrine slid his arm under Dora's waist so he could draw her closer to him. She turned onto her side and brushed a fluttering kiss against his cheek, setting another wave of longing in motion.

"Is there something I could do differently?" he asked.

"What if'—she hesitated for a moment—"are there positions where I could control how we moved?"

"Yes, of course." He ought to have thought of that. He rolled onto his back. "Why don't you sit on top of me? Then you can move however you like. I lost some of my hardness, though," he confessed. "Do you mind helping me with that first?"

Dora nodded, so he put her hand where he wanted it. It took only a few teasing strokes to return the firmness to his cockstand. But her touch felt so good that he let her keep moving her hand up and down until he could no longer stand the hot ache.

"That's enough," he rasped. "Can we—?"

She did not need him to complete the sentence. "Yes," she said.

He helped guide her into position. She slowly lowered herself down, inch by teasing inch. He squeezed his eyes shut and forced himself to be patient, though he desperately wanted to be surrounded by her heat again. When she fully engulfed him, she made a few experimental movements back and forth, then up and down.

"How does that feel?" he asked anxiously. As much as he longed to lose himself in pleasure, he did not want to do so at Dora's expense.

"It doesn't hurt. But it doesn't feel particularly good, if you know what I mean." Her lips stuck out in a pout.

"What if I do this?" He cautiously circled the sensitive spot at the front of her quim with his thumb.

She sighed in response to his touch. "Yes, that's good," she murmured. "But a little slower—yes, like that."

After that, he had no need for further instruction. As Dora moved back and forth, grinding against his hand, he watched her face for clues on when to speed up, when to press more firmly. He felt her ecstasy before she made any sound, as the muscles in her core clenched rhythmically around him. She spent herself with a soft moan that sent shivers down his spine.

"That was *good*," she murmured.

A grin broke across his face. "I am glad to hear that." And rather proud of himself.

Dora opened her eyes and looked down at him. "What about you? Do you want to switch positions again?"

"No. But move a little more slowly and, um,"—he scrambled frantically for the words; his vocabulary on this subject was entirely inadequate—"longer movements back and forth. Like a long, slow slide."

"Like this?" she said.

He answered her with only a desperate whine. When he caught his breath, he begged: "More, please."

Fortunately, she did not need any more direction than that. She kept up the slow, firm movement until he could stand it no more. He took hold of her hips so he could take charge of the movement himself, thrusting more quickly until he finally reached his release. He finished with a quiet sigh, letting his whole body relax.

When he finally opened his eyes, Dora was smiling down at him. The corners of his mouth automatically curled in response. "How was that?" she asked him.

His smile broadened into a full grin. "I think you know the answer. You are intelligent enough to figure out for yourself that it was very good."

She laughed and collapsed on him. He rested his face against her head. Her cropped hair tickled against his cheek, but it was not an unpleasant sensation.

"I can already tell that I am going to like being married," she announced.

For once, he was the one who broke into laughter. "You aren't the only one," he assured her. Taking Dora to bed was every bit as good as he'd imagined, and he suspected it would just get better in the future, as they figured out how to please each other.

Warmed by that thought, he closed his eyes and let himself slide from happiness into sleep.

CHAPTER TWENTY-ONE

THE DAY AFTER their wedding, Dora woke early. Birds were already singing, but the sky was still rosy with dawn. Peregrine slumbered, the blanket wrapped tightly about him. As she studied her husband, a sudden flush of affection warmed her from head to toe, bringing tears to her eyes.

She blinked her tears away. There was nothing to cry about. Peregrine was her husband now. Now, no one could keep them apart: not her interfering Grantly relatives, not the court of Chancery, not the ridiculous conventions of proper courtship, no one. They were firmly bound together. They were *married*.

She did not want to wake Peregrine from his peaceful rest, so she leaned down and kissed his cheek so softly, she barely felt the touch. Then she got out of bed and began rooting through the contents of her valise.

Dora did not feel the least bit sleepy, and she could not sit still on such a glorious June morning. What she needed was a proper walk. She could clamber over a fence into someone's pasture— preferably one not occupied by irate cattle—and expend some of this restless energy in with a hearty cross-country ramble.

She had already started pulling on her trousers before it dawned on her that there would be complications if she walked out of the room dressed in men's clothing. She had not checked into the inn as Mr. Rossini, but as Miss Rossini—no, she corrected herself, she had checked in as Mrs. Carrington!

Mrs. Carrington. She cautiously turned the name over in her mind. It did not sound right. *Carrington* was such a dignified, genteel name, but she was neither dignified nor genteel. She could not be Mrs. Carrington, could she? She had been Miss Rossini all her life.

In England, all women gave up their surname when they married. No doubt many of them found the experience puzzling. But Dora doubted most new brides felt as conflicted as she did. Her surname was almost the only thing her mother had left to her, apart from a cask of expensive jewelry (gifts from Sir Isaac) that remained locked in a safe at Grantly Manor. Of the two inheritances, she treasured her surname more.

The name Rossini had set her apart from her half siblings. When Dora was a child, that had troubled her. Once, she'd longed to be addressed as Miss Dora Grantly, so there would be no distinction between her and her siblings. So no one would know she was an outsider in her own home. Once, it had been the dream of her heart that Sir Isaac would publicly acknowledge her as his daughter and lend her the dignity of his own name.

But in her teens, Dora took apart all her conceptions of her own identity and the surrounding social order, then reassembled them in an arrangement that made much better sense. Honora, who always knew the right questions to ask, had helped her do it. By the end of this rather painful process, she'd emerged proud of being Dora Rossini.

Must she become Mrs. Carrington, then? She stared at her sleeping husband. She had no desire to deny her relationship to him. She loved Peregrine and was proud to be his wife. But what had happened to Dora Rossini? Was her past to be lost forever? She shook her head, not yet having any answers. Then she reluctantly stripped off her trousers and donned yesterday's walking dress.

In some situations, skirts could be more comfortable than pantaloons, but Dora preferred not having to worry about dirtying the hem of her gown. Boots and trousers were far more practical for tramping over hills, across pastures, or even along dirty roads. Moreover, a young man could roam about the country lanes and fields with more freedom than a young lady could. Theo Rossini would attract less notice than Dora Carrington.

But Dora already had enough on her mind this morning. She did not want to have to figure out how to sneak in and out of the inn dressed like a man. The innkeeper and tavern maid had seen her arrive and knew her to be a bride. Unless she pretended to have a twin brother, there would be many questions if she were caught in men's clothing. Another day, she might have taken the risk. But it had been an eventful week and she was not quite running on full steam.

Switching from trousers to a skirt complicated her planned hike, though. In the end, she contented herself with walking sedately down the road to one end of town, then back the other way. She lost count of how many laps she did before she came to a decision, but she suspected it was a lot, given the way the hostlers stared at her when she finally returned to the inn.

She'd feared Peregrine might still be asleep at this hour, but she found him shaving in front of a small traveling mirror. She sat on the bed and watched him work in silence, suspecting he would not like being disturbed in such a delicate task.

He put down his straight razor and smiled at her. "You are up early."

"I felt restless," she admitted. "I had some thinking to do."

"Oh, I know that feeling. Sometimes nothing but a brisk walk can untangle my thoughts." He picked up a comb and began to tidy his bed-mussed hair. "Did you figure things out?"

"I think so." She clasped her hands and steeled herself for disappointment. "Peregrine—what would you say if I asked you to change your name?"

His eyes widened, and he put the comb back down on the dressing table. But he did not scowl or frown or look aghast—merely surprised. She drew in a slow, deep breath, hardly daring to hope.

"Change it to what?" he asked.

"Carrington-Rossini. Or Rossini-Carrington. I suppose the order does not matter." She swallowed nervously, wishing she had a cup of tea to help clear her throat. Perhaps it was a mistake to have this conversation before breakfast. "Sometimes people do combine their names, you know, when . . . when two families unite."

She fell silent, knowing perfectly well how ridiculous it was to apply that tradition to their case. Wealthy people sometimes hyphenated their names when there was no male heir to preserve the surname of an illustrious family. When an estate passed down the female line, it was not uncommon to request a man to change his surname so the heiress's family name would not be lost. Had Peregrine married an heiress from a prestigious family, it might have made sense for him to change his name. But Dora was not wealthy and there was nothing prestigious about her mother's family, so far as she knew.

"Oh, yes," he agreed. "In Germany, they call those *Allianznamen*. Alliance names. I had not thought about it, but I suppose it would be more logical for both of us to change our names than for only you to do so. And since I am only a second son, it is not as if I am needed to carry on the Carrington name." Now he did frown. "At least, not if Amelia's next baby is a boy. Things might get complicated if Roderick does not have a male heir."

"That's right. You would be the next baronet if Roderick does not have a son." She had forgotten that. Roderick and his wife were both young, so it seemed an unlikely contingency, but even young people sometimes died unexpectedly. "I suppose you could always change your name back to Carrington, if need be."

"I had rather not be baronet at all, but if that happened, I could just as easily be Sir Peregrine Carrington-Rossini, couldn't I?" He wrinkled his nose. "Rather a mouthful, isn't it? Let's hope that the next Carrington infant inherits instead. I have a perfectly adequate inheritance of my own, after all. I don't need to inherit the family estate, too."

"Indeed not," Dora agreed. The fortune Peregrine had been left by his great-uncle seemed more than "adequate" to her. His income allowed him to socialize on equal footing with members of the landed gentry, though he had no country estate of his own. "Then you'll consider it?"

"Consider it?" He wrinkled his brow in confusion. "I thought we had already settled it! We will be Mr. and Mrs. Carrington-Rossini. Or Rossini-Carrington, if you prefer that."

"Oh, we can put your name first," Dora said magnanimously. He was the one making a concession, after all. Besides, she thought it sounded better that way, though she could not have said why. "Yes, it is settled." She bounced up and down, relieved to have that weighty matter so easily resolved.

"I assume that we should depart right after breakfast?" Peregrine suggested.

Dora stared at him blankly. "Oh, are we not staying here?" When his eyes widened, she hurried to explain. "I thought we might as well honeymoon in Scotland, now that we're here." She had never been this far north before. What was to stop them from traveling farther? They could easily visit Glasgow before they went back to England.

A thoughtful wrinkle appeared on his brow. "I don't like leaving things with Mr. Blithfield unsettled. He must wonder what happened to me. And I want to pick up my things. I don't have a change of clothes, you know."

"Oh, right!" She had forgotten that. For that matter, she did not have an extensive wardrobe with her, either. She only had the one dress. And if she was to travel with Peregrine as his wife, she could not very well run about in pantaloons and Hessian boots, more's the pity. "I suppose we had better go back to Cumberland, then."

"If you like," he suggested, "we could tour the Lake District for a week or two before we go to Carrington Abbey. We don't have to be in Surrey until Midsummer."

She brightened. "Yes, let's do that."

True, she had not packed for a long journey, but maybe she could find a dressmaker with stock on hand that fit her—though she was rather a difficult shape to fit, not having the large bosom favored by current fashion. But Peregrine did not seem to mind that, and neither did she. It would have been harder to disguise herself as Theo Rossini had she been more curvaceous.

Breakfast was at least more satisfying than last night's dinner. The inn served black pudding, tattie scones, and sausage, as well as porridge. Dora tried some of everything; Peregrine stuck to the scones and sausage.

"You never know what's in those puddings." He shook his head.

Dora ignored his pessimism and ended up eating so much that she fell asleep on the drive back to Carlisle. She woke up feeling both thirsty and groggy.

"Why don't you stay here and have a cup of tea or a bite of luncheon?" Peregrine suggested. "I will nip over to Corbin Hall, get my things, and. . ." His voice faltered.

"Make your apologies?" she suggested.

"It is going to be hard to explain, isn't it?" he said wistfully.

"Do you want me to make up a lie for you?" Dora offered. "For instance, you could tell Mr. Blithfield that your younger brother ran off with a schoolgirl and you had to chase them down—"

"Cosmo would never do that!" Peregrine sounded horrified. "He doesn't even like women. Or men, for that matter. Just math."

Dora closed her eyes and counted to three, summoning her patience. "But Mr. Blithfield doesn't know that, does he? So it could still work. But if you don't like that idea, say something else. Tell him your sister is dying of consumption, and sinking quickly!" Tuberculosis of the lungs was a stubborn disease that could not always be cured even by magic.

"No," he said flatly. He furrowed his brow as he thought for a moment. "I will tell him that my betrothed—no, that my wife showed up unexpectedly with . . . news . . . of some sort."

Dora snorted. For all his brilliance, Peregrine sometimes lacked imagination. "I could make up a much better story than that."

Peregrine jutted his chin out. "I don't see why an elaborate fiction is necessary," he argued. "I will tell him that I was called away on very important family matters. That is the truth, in a way. I mean, getting married is important, isn't it?"

Dora paused to consider all the dramatic possibilities. "That might do," she agreed. "Especially if you look very distraught and act as if something unspeakably terrible has happened." She began to warm up to the idea. Everyone would, naturally, wonder what terrible thing had happened, and the mystery would plague them. That would be a just punishment for Mr. Blithfield's perfidy.

Her husband shook his head. "I think it will be best if I keep things simple. I don't want to lie more than I have to."

And that, Dora thought, was the difference between them. She enjoyed a well-crafted falsehood as long as the lie worked as intended. Peregrine had rather tell the truth, even if doing so made life more difficult. Most of the time his honesty was more endearing than not, but she worried that in this situation, it might be a liability.

"I suppose you can make your excuses without telling any blatant falsehoods," she agreed. "The reason for your departure isn't really any of Mr. Blithfield's business, is it?" A good host would not want to prevent his guest from leaving in an emergency.

"Exactly!" Peregrine sounded more cheerful. "I will simply explain that I have been called away, get my things, and leave as quickly as I can. Politely, of course. When I get back, we can work out where to go next."

Dora brightened. She already had ideas about that. "We should go to Keswick, where Mr. Coleridge used to live." She was not particularly fond of poetry, but it might be fun to see the old stomping grounds of the Lake School poets. "I could ask the innkeeper if he can recommend a hostelry there. That will give me something to do while you are away."

She might as well inquire if the innkeeper knew where she could buy a change of clothing, too. Surely someone in Carlisle sold used clothing? She would have to hurry, though. Peregrine's errand would probably take no more than a couple of hours.

CHAPTER TWENTY-TWO

P EREGRINE DREADED THE return to Corbin Hall. Blithfield and his other guests would certainly have questions for him. In order to answer those questions, he would have to skirt the fine line between truth and fabrication. Dora might be good at this sort of thing, but he most certainly was not. If only she could have gone in his place!

In one regard, he lucked out: He arrived during the afternoon recreation hours, so most of the guests were out and about. They were probably fishing or walking or napping rather than sitting in the drawing room vigorously debating some fine point of magical theory.

The butler informed Peregrine that Mr. Blithfield wanted to see him as soon as possible. "I believe he is in the study at this hour, sir," he suggested.

Peregrine took the hint and went looking for his host. Mr. Blithfield turned out to be in the billiard room, which also served as a make-shift laboratory. Under normal conditions, this was probably a comfortable game room, particularly when a fire crackled on the hearth. Now, with the carpet rolled back and cluttered worktables scattered around the room, it looked so businesslike that the billiard table seemed out of place. Blithfield and Turnbull, playing billiards in their shirtsleeves while surrounded by all the paraphernalia of wizardry, looked downright surreal.

Blithfield put down his cue stick the moment he saw Peregrine. "Ah, Mr. Carrington! I am glad to see you in good health. You had us very worried, you know."

Peregrine squared his shoulders in preparation for what might be a difficult conversation. "I am very sorry for any distress I may have caused. Something came up." As soon as the words were out of his mouth, he realized how inane they sounded. That was no explanation at all. "Some important family matters." That was not much better, was it?

"Ah, if you'll excuse me, I just remembered something I have to do," Mr. Turnbull announced. He put down his cue and hurried out of the room. Peregrine stared after him, surprised by his sudden departure.

"Family matters?" Mr. Blithfield drew his brows together, though Peregrine could not tell if he was unhappy or merely confused. "I didn't know you had family in the area."

"Oh, it is quite complicated." Peregrine stretched his mouth into a smile that probably looked as unnatural as it felt. "I am very sorry to do this, but I am afraid I must—" His voice trailed off. Must what? He was not, after all, going back to London, but he could hardly admit that he planned to honeymoon by Derwentwater.

He cleared his throat and floundered on. "I must take my leave. To, er . . ." To take his wife to bed as often as he could. But he could not say that, either, even though it was true. "To deal with important matters," Peregrine concluded. "I am very grateful for your hospitality, Mr. Blithfield." He probably ought to offer to come to next year's gathering, too, but he could not bring himself to say that. He would prefer never to see Blithfield or his friends again.

Blithfield frowned and rubbed his chin. "I am sorry to hear you are leaving us so soon, Mr. Carrington. I don't suppose there is anything I can do to convince you to stay?"

"No," Peregrine blurted out. "I really must go. So very sorry." He sighed, because his excuses did not sound convincing even to him. "It is a most unexpected family situation."

Unexpected really was the best word for it. Peregrine had never expected Dora to come running after him, and he certainly had not anticipated that she would want to get married at a moment's notice. Not that he had any objection.

True, Peregrine generally preferred to plan things out in advance rather than doing them spontaneously. But, he reasoned, it was not as if Dora could possibly make a habit of spontaneously marrying him. Having dealt with that unexpected situation once, he need never worry about it happening again.

"Well, Mr. Carrington, far be it from me to keep you from your family in an emergency." Blithfield rocked back and forth on his heels, still rubbing his chin thoughtfully. "But before you go, there's something I wanted to ask you."

"Yes?" Peregrine's whole body felt lighter now that they'd gotten past the most awkward part of the conversation. He would happily answer any questions of Blithfield's, provided he could do so without betraying anyone else's confidence.

Mr. Blithfield smiled—and something in the room shifted. For a startling moment, Peregrine thought he was in the middle of an earthquake, because it felt as if the ground rippled beneath his feet. But, to his confusion, nothing else in the room was moving with him. Not even the billiard balls, which should have been rolling about the table if something had actually shaken the foundations of the house.

If the house wasn't shaking, why was Peregrine's head swimming? He shook his head, as if that could rattle some sense back into him. It did not help. On the contrary, he felt even more dizzy.

"I am very sorry," he said, "but I am feeling most unwell just now." Could it have been something he ate? He didn't trust the food at the inn in Gretna Green.

"Perhaps you ought to defer your journey." Blithfield moved closer and put a hand on Peregrine's shoulder. He probably meant to help, but Peregrine jerked away from him, horrified by the unexpected touch. "You do look unwell, Mr. Carrington."

"I must get back to Dora," Peregrine said. The moment the words were out of his mouth, he wondered why he'd spoken them. Up until now he had avoided mentioning Dora. He certainly hadn't named her.

"Dora?" Blithfield tilted his head to one side. "I had not thought you the sort of man to keep a ladybird, Mr. Carrington. But I suppose you never can tell, can you? Well, your light o' love will have to wait a little longer. There are things I need to ask you."

Peregrine gritted his teeth. There were things he needed to say, too, but he could not. Literally could not, because the pressure in his head made it impossible to speak. This was not an illness, he realized. This was mind magic.

Of course. Blithfield was a mage, wasn't he? Peregrine had forgotten that. It had been easy to forget, because all throughout the house party, Blithefield spent his time encouraging other magicians, listening to them, and helping them find the materials they needed for their work. He had never demonstrated any of his own magic. Peregrine had assumed that was because he did not have much magical ability. Now he had to rethink that. Blithfield seemed to have a good deal of power. He had simply chosen not to advertise it.

"What I need from you, Mr. Carrington," Blithfield continued, "is the latest version of your meteor trap. You can write it out or dictate it to me, whichever you prefer. But I need all the details—enough to work the enchantment." He lifted his hand, palm up, and slowly began to close it. The force of his spell increased as his hand tightened into a fist.

Every joint in Peregrine's body stiffened. Some of his shock arose from the intense pressure of the mind magic, but some of it was pure rage. He was not sure he'd ever been this angry in his life. There were some things a gentleman-scholar simply did not do!

"You can't steal my spell," he sputtered. "I'm not finished

fine-tuning it!" It wasn't *ready* to be stolen yet! Not that he would have wanted it to be stolen at any point in the future, but it certainly would have made more sense for Blithfield to wait until it was completely finished to steal it.

"You need not worry about that any longer." Strangely, Blithfield used a soothing voice rather than an adversarial one. "My team will handle all of that. Between the lot of us, we have a good deal of magical expertise. You would be surprised what we can accomplish working together! All you need to do is tell me your latest changes."

Peregrine shook his head. Gestures seemed easier than speech, given the pressure of Blithfield's magecraft.

Blithfield frowned. "I did not expect you to be so resistant. You have always seemed an easygoing man, despite your eccentricities."

"I am not easygoing when people insult my wife and try to steal my work!" Peregrine snapped back.

Blithfield raised his eyebrows. "A wife rather than a mistress, then? My mistake." He shrugged his shoulders with a casual insolence that infuriated Peregrine. "I was under the impression that you were a bachelor. Well, Mr. Carrington, as soon as you give me the current version of the spell, I will let you go." He twisted his mouth into a malicious smile. "After I modify your memories, that is."

"That," Peregrine hissed, "is illegal." Invasively reading thoughts was considered a moral gray area in magical circles, but the law of Great Britain made it very clear that *tampering* with other people's thoughts was a crime.

Mr. Blithfield shrugged. "It's not illegal if no one finds out."

Peregrine scoffed. That was not, in fact, how the law worked. But he had other objections, too. "Everyone who studies astronomical magic knows that Dora and I wrote the spell. You can't fool the people who matter."

"They know you wrote the original spell, yes," Blithfield agreed. "But they will think one of us is responsible for the modifications. And you will not be able to tell them otherwise, because you will not remember any of this."

Peregrine sucked in his breath. Blithfield could tamper with memories? That required difficult mind magic, and it could be hard to control the extent of the memory loss. But Blithfield had already shown that he was both powerful and unethical. Peregrine wouldn't put it past him.

Good heavens, was *that* what had happened to Ned Anderson last summer? Peregrine's stomach roiled. The thought of Ned's weather spells—even his memory of them—being stolen was heartbreaking, but it would explain so much. Poor Ned!

Meanwhile, Blithfield kept talking. "I suppose I had better do something about your wife, too. Can't have her running around contradicting my story. Most people would not believe a woman anyway, but—"

"No," Peregrine snapped. He crossed his arms in front of his chest and drew himself to his full height. "You won't do a thing to Dora. If you so much as try to touch her, you will regret it."

Mr. Blithfield chuckled. "Threatening me now, are you? Goodness, you do have hidden depths!"

Peregrine did not hear a word Blithfield said after that. He was too busy scanning the room for anything he could use against Blithfield. He might not have brought ingredients for his magic with him, but, the room was full of *materia magica* just waiting to be used.

Peregrine took a few slow steps backwards, edging closer to a worktable covered with apothecary jars. Unfortunately, these jars contained nothing more dangerous than cooking ingredients. Had someone been making spice cake?

That's when a bolt of panicked brilliance struck Peregrine. Cooking spices had other uses, too, didn't they? He took a final step closer to the table, reached behind him, and closed his hand around what he hoped was a jar of nutmeg.

Mr. Blithfield laughed. "You can threaten all you want, but you are outnumbered, Mr. Carrington. You see, I do not work alone, and—" He broke off and gaped at Peregrine. "What are you doing?"

Peregrine saw no reason to lie. "I'm just opening a jar of nutmeg." Doing so with his hands behind his back had been quite awkward, but he hadn't wanted his plan to be too obvious. He need not have worried. Mr. Blithfield still looked completely baffled.

"Nutmeg? Why in the world would you—"

"I need it for a spell," Peregrine explained. He threw the jar at Mr. Blithfield, and just before it hit, he said "*Perturbo*," keeping his voice cool and collected. Magic worked best when one remained calm.

Which was precisely why his disruption spell was so effective. Nutmeg was poisonous in large quantities; it could cause confusion and hallucinations. That made it the perfect ingredient for a disruption spell where the magic magnified and extended the herb's natural properties.

Blithfield had clearly not anticipated such an attack, though he ought to have realized that confronting a wizard in a room full of magical supplies was a bad idea. He stumbled backwards, covering his eyes with hands. But it was too late. Peregrine had already felt the spell take.

"I am going to report you to the Home Office," Peregrine informed Blithfield.

The Department of Magical Regulation would be interested to learn that Blitfhield and his friends had been stealing other people's magical inventions. It wouldn't hurt that the current minister was one of Peregrine's cousins. Not a close cousin, true, but they'd met once or twice. He would most likely remember Peregrine, since Peregrine had accidentally turned him purple at their first encounter.

Mr. Blithfield paid no attention to Peregrine's threat. He may not even have heard it. By now, he'd collapsed onto the floor. He still sat upright, but he leaned awkwardly against the leg of the billiard table, holding his head in his hands.

"I must bid you good day," Peregrine said. Though he worried a little about the effects of his confusion spell, but he preferred not to linger.

Most fortuitously, he encountered the butler just outside the billiard room. "If you please," Peregrine said, "I wish to have all of my possessions packed up and forwarded to this address." He handed the servant his card.

The butler's mouth fell open in very unprofessional surprise. "You wish your things shipped to London, sir? But—"

"Yes." He dug in his pocket and found a sovereign. It would, after all, cost money to ship a trunk so far. "I am afraid I must leave in rather a hurry." The longer he lingered, the greater the chance that Blithfield might recover in time to raise the alarm.

The butler looked past Peregrine to someone approaching from the other end of the hall. "Ah, sir. Perhaps you can help? Mr. Carrington needs to take his leave."

Peregrine twisted his neck trying to see who had snuck up behind him, but before he could get a good look, the stranger said *"Dormi."*

Something cold and wet splashed against Peregrine's jacket, stinging him with magic. Very little of the potion touched his bare skin, but just enough must have made contact, because his eyelids grew heavy. Then the whole world tilted sideways as he tumbled into a magical sleep.

CHAPTER TWENTY-THREE

Finding clothes that fit turned out to be easier than Dora anticipated. The innkeeper's wife's cousin worked as a dressmaker, and she quickly rustled up a few lightly used gowns. She brought these to the inn so that Dora could try them on. None of them fit perfectly, but Dora found a walking dress and an evening dress that would do well enough, under the circumstances.

After paying the seamstress, Dora hurried to the nearest milliner to buy a better bonnet. The hat she'd brought with her was rather worse for being crammed into a valise instead of carried in a proper hatbox. There were a number of charming hats in the shop, but she snatched up the first suitable one she found. She didn't want to keep Peregrine waiting.

But she need not have hurried after all. Peregrine was not back, though he surely ought to have been. She wondered what could be keeping him, but she set the thought aside while she repacked her valise. Saying his good-byes probably took longer than he'd expected. She saw no need to worry.

Until the chaise Peregrine had hired came back without him.

"Where is my husband?" she asked the postilion.

He shrugged. "At the hall, I s'pose. I was only told that the chaise weren't needed after all."

Dora frowned. "Mr. Carrington told you that?"

He shook his head. "No, ma'am."

She started at the word *ma'am*. Until now, she had always been addressed as *miss*. She'd forgotten that would change now that she was a married woman.

The young man continued speaking. "It was one of the gentlemen at the hall as spoke to me. I dunno his name, but he said Mr. Carrington had changed his mind and was going to stay on at the hall."

"Bullshit." Dora had picked up that profanity from her brother-in-law. She could see that her language shocked the postilion, but she did not care. *She* thought the word fit this situation very well. "My husband gave you no message to pass on to me?"

"No, ma'am. I didn't speak to him at all. Is there anything more you wish to know?" He shuffled his feet nervously, looking like he wanted to escape.

"That is all, thank you," Dora said.

She went in search of the innkeeper. He had been watching with an anxious face from the doorway of the inn. He could probably tell something was wrong.

"Is there some way that I can assist you, ma'am?" he offered. "Send a message for you, perhaps?" The worry in his face colored his voice, too.

Did he think her husband had abandoned her? Dora wondered. That was bullshit, too. Peregrine would never do that. Not on purpose, anyway. She could not vouch for what would happen if someone lured him away with the promise of an interesting meteorite to look at. But she felt confident that even if Peregrine became temporarily distracted, he would eventually make his way back to her.

Maybe that was all that had happened today. Possibly one of the other magicians at Corbin Hall had shared something interesting with Peregrine. But she worried he might have been detained by something more threatening than a particularly fascinating magical discovery.

"Actually," she said, "I wondered if you have a gig I could borrow."

"A gig?" The innkeeper's eyes widened.

"I am afraid my husband may have met with some mischance," she explained. "It is not like him to change his plans without sending me any notice. I wish to go look for him."

He pursed his lips. "Can you drive a gig yourself, madam?"

Dora supposed he was right to wonder. She was a proficient rider, but had only handled the reins of a horse in harness once or twice. She was not afraid to try, but maybe it wasn't fair to experiment with someone else's equipage. That might be a recipe for disaster.

"I suppose not," she admitted. "But I would be happy to reimburse one of the grooms for their time."

"My grooms are busy," the innkeeper said, "but my son knows how to drive a cart right enough, and he is not busy just now. He'll take you to Corbin Hall and back, madam."

"Thank you," Dora said. "And . . . I don't suppose I could borrow a butcher knife, too?"

His eyes flew wide open. "*A knife?*" he squeaked.

"Just in case." She smiled as if this were a perfectly reasonable request, and hoped her confidence would win the day. Creative though she might be, even she could think of no plausible explanation for taking a knife with her.

Whatever the innkeeper may have suspected, he did not refuse her request. He gave her something better than a butcher knife: a clasp knife small enough to fit into her reticule. With that on hand, she felt she could more confidently face whatever might have detained her husband.

Dora was armed with something even better than a knife, too: her gift of sorcery. Most young ladies were never taught combat magic. But after Dora had heard one too many thrilling stories about housebreakers and highwaymen, she asked her father what she should do if ever someone attacked her. Rather than scoff at her fears, Sir Isaac had taught her spells both to shield herself and to temporarily incapacitate an assailant. She had never had cause to use any of those spells, but she had engrained them in her memory.

Half an hour later, she was rolling along the road, holding a borrowed parasol over her head to protect her face from the sun. The innkeeper's son proved to be a shy towheaded lad who spoke only to point out wildflowers they passed along the way. They had a good deal of time to talk about wildflowers, because the nag pulling the gig shuffled along at a lazy trot.

Finally, they drew in front of Corbin Hall. Dora studied it, squinting her eyes against the late afternoon light. It was a handsome stone building. She did not know enough about architecture to recognize the style, but she guessed it had been built only a century or two ago. Certainly, it did not look nearly as old as Carrington Abbey, which had seen kings, bishops, and whole religious communities pass by.

"Do you want me to wait for you, miss?" The boy yawned and leaned back against the seat, as if prepared to rest regardless of her answer.

"If you can wait half an hour, I would much appreciate that," she said. "If you do not hear from me by then, send for help."

"Help?" His eyes, which had been half shut against the sunlight, flew open.

"Just in case." Once again, Dora refrained from elaborating in case of *what*. She had no idea what might have gone wrong at Corbin Hall, but she felt very certain that something was amiss.

Time to find some answers.

The butler did not want to admit her. "I am very sorry ma'am, but Mr. Blithfield is indisposed. He is not accepting visitors. You had better come back tomorrow."

"My mission is urgent. It cannot wait." Dora performed her very best imitation of Lady Grantly, fixing the butler with a glare so steely, he visibly flinched.

What do you know—apparently, she *had* learned something of use from her evil stepmother! Over the years, Dora had plenty of opportunity to study the art of Getting Your Own Way. Being a keen scholar, she'd paid attention.

The butler yielded to the sheer force of Dora's determination. "You may wait in the blue salon if you like," he conceded. "But I doubt that anyone can you see you today, ma'am."

"I will wait," Dora said majestically. At least, she hoped she sounded majestic. She was built on much slighter lines than Lady Grantly, and she did not have the latter's title to back her up. Hopefully she could make up for that lack with personality. She had loads of that.

She did not, in fact, wait in the blue salon. Not for one minute. As soon as the butler's footsteps had receded down the corridor, she closed her eyes and cast a simple finding spell. She was bound to Peregrine by physical, emotional, and legal ties. Such affinity made it easy to locate him. The spell tugged her up two flights of stairs and down a corridor to a locked bedroom.

Today, Dora had no patience for locks. She put her hand on the knob, whispered "Open Sesame," and sent her magic into the lock. When she countered unexpected magical resistance, she pushed harder. Whoever locked this door had possessed a good deal of power, but Dora was not in the mood to be trifled with. The spell gave in with a final sizzle of magic, and the lock opened with a click.

Behind the door lay a small bedchamber, empty of everything but a bed. Peregrine lay on that bed, sleeping so soundly that a thread of drool wandered down his cheek. That put a grin on Dora's face, but her smile faded the moment she rested a hand on his shoulder. This was not a natural sleep: He had been sedated by a spell.

Dora's heart ached with worry, but she pushed her fear aside. She gently shook Peregrine's shoulder. "Love," she whispered. "You need to wake up."

She'd thought she might need magic to break the spell, but, to her relief, her voice and touch were enough to rouse Peregrine.

He opened his eyes and yawned. "Oh, is it time to get up?" he murmured sleepily. "Did I oversleep?"

She had no idea how to answer that, so she skipped straight to the point. "We need to get you out of here before they do something worse to you."

Peregrine sat up and wiped the drool off his face. "Worse than what? Mr. Blithfield tried to steal our latest modifications to the meteorite spell."

"Well, that wouldn't have been very successful, because you don't even know some of the changes I've made to the sorcerous part of the enchantment," Dora grumbled. She'd kept tinkering with her part of the spell while Peregrine was away, and she'd made some real progress.

His eyes brightened. "Oh, really? Did you figure out how to limit—"

"This is not the time to discuss our work," she interrupted She did not have the patience to explain her revisions to the spell. "We need to get you out of here."

Peregrine sighed. "I suppose you're right. You can tell me about it later. After we talk to the local magistrate."

"Magistrate?" She hadn't thought of that. "Oh, right, it's against the law to detain someone against their will." Using magic made the crime worse, since it was misuse of magic as well as unlawful restraint.

"I was thinking more of the fact that they were trying to steal my intellectual property," Peregrine explained, "but I should probably mention the part about them using sorcery to keep me here."

"Yes, I think you should." Dora said drily. She suspected most magistrates would care more about kidnapping charges than about someone trying to claim another person's spell as their own work. People outside the magical community might not realize how devastating plagiarism could be.

"But now we should get out of here. I have a gig waiting—at least, I think it's still waiting." It couldn't have been half an hour already, could it? Goodness, she hoped not.

Peregrine got to his feet and stretched. "Yes, let's leave. I have had enough of this house party. The food wasn't even that good. The cook here has been influenced too much by the fad for French cuisine."

Dora's shoulders shook with suppressed laughter. Of all the things to complain about, that *would* be what stuck out to Peregrine!

But her urge to laugh dissipated like dandelion fluff when someone flung open the door to the bedroom. A tall, sturdy man of middle years blocked the doorway.

He drew his brows down into an impressive scowl as he stared at Dora. "Who are you? What are you doing here?"

CHAPTER TWENTY-FOUR

"A H, MR. TURNBULL, I wondered if we'd see you again." Peregrine could not be certain, but he thought Turnbull had been the one to put him under the sleeping spell. That made him an enemy. "You'll have to excuse us, as we were just leaving." He stepped closer to Dora so it would be clear that they were together.

"I don't think you're going anywhere." Turnbull lifted his left hand, revealing that he was armed with a wand.

Dora flinched. Peregrine put a hand on her shoulder and squeezed it lightly to reassure her. But the sight of the wand rattled him, too. Wizards used wands to store spells for future use; it meant they didn't have to carry all the ingredients for a spell with them. Judging from the threatening way Turnbull brandished the wand, Peregrine guessed he'd loaded it with rather nasty magic.

"I am afraid I do have to leave," Peregrine told Mr. Turnbull. "There's, ah, a rather urgent situation we must attend to." Namely, they had to report these criminal activities to the nearest magistrate. "This house party really has been . . . something. Something interesting. Interesting in ways I couldn't have imagined." As Turnbull's glare deepened, Peregrine quit babbling. Better to just shut up!

Turnbull flicked his eyes in Dora's direction. "I don't know who you are, young lady, but you are interfering in a very complicated situation. You probably don't realize this, but Mr. Carrington is very ill. He has"—he cast his eyes around the room, as if searching for inspiration—"a terrible fever, and it is making him delirious."

"I do not have a fever!" Peregrine protested. "And I am not delirious. My brain is working perfectly well right now, thank you very much." True, he could do with a strong cup of tea. But he felt no foggier than he normally did upon waking.

Dora snorted. "There was nothing wrong with Mr. Carrington except that he'd been put into a magical sleep. Did he give you permission to cast that spell? Working medical magic without a patient's consent is illegal, you know—"

"Consent is not needed when a person is incapacitated," Turnbull retorted. "As I said, Mr. Carrington is *very* ill. I am afraid, miss, that he is not in his right mind. We are waiting for a physician to examine him, but I must warn you that he has resisted any attempts at treatment."

"Because I'm not ill!" Peregrine retorted. This was ridiculous. Anyone who examined him could tell he did not have a fever. "What symptoms do I display?"

Turnbull shook his head solemnly. "Derangement, incoherence, claims of a conspiracy against him. All symptoms of brain fever."

Peregrine opened his mouth, intending to explain that there really *was* a conspiracy against him, which meant that didn't count as a symptom. Dora spoke before he could get a word out.

"He seems perfectly coherent to me. In any case, as his wife, I am his next of kin. If he is ill, it is my responsibility to see that he gets the medical care he needs. I am going to take him into Carlisle to see a physician now." She took Peregrine by the hand. This time, she was the one to give him a reassuring squeeze.

"His wife?" Turnbull was so startled that he unwisely lowered his wand. "Mr. Carrington isn't married."

"I wasn't married yesterday morning," Peregrine explained, "but I am now." Too late, it occurred to him that his explanation might support Turnbull's claim that he was incoherent. "We went to Scotland, you see. All perfectly in order."

Turnbull shook his head, looking dazed by this unexpected development.

Dora took advantage of his momentary confusion to act. "It was very pleasant to meet you, Mr. What's-Your-Name. But I am afraid we really can't stay. People to see, crimes to report, you know how it is! *Dormi statim.*"

She snapped her fingers to set in motion an accelerated version of the very spell that had been used on Peregrine. It took effect immediately. First the wand tumbled from Turnbull's suddenly clumsy fingers, then his whole body slumped. He collapsed onto the floor, as sound asleep as Peregrine had been a quarter of an hour ago.

But he deserved such treatment, in Peregrine's opinion. Stupid of him not to have suspected that Dora was a magician! If Turnbull had paid attention to Peregrine's presentation last week, he would have known Peregrine had a partner who worked sorcery. It probably never occurred to him that the sorcerer might be a woman.

Dora walked over to Turnbull and poked him with the toe of her boot. He did not so much as a twitch.

She nodded in satisfaction. "I'm going to have a nasty headache after that, though," she complained.

"Too much magic at once, hmm?" Peregrine murmured sympathetically. Medical magic was not Dora's specialty, so he was impressed she had been able to work the spell at all. "Maybe the Silver Griffin keeps chocolate on hand." Any sugary food could be helpful after one magically overextended oneself, but chocolate was a particularly effective anecdote to magical exertion. No one knew why.

"A cup of tea with sugar is more likely." Dora sounded resigned. She was probably right: drinking chocolate was a luxury, and the Silver Griffin was not a particularly luxurious hostelry.

"We should go before the boy with the gig abandons us," she

said.

He had no objection to following her. As far as Peregrine was concerned, the sooner they could leave, the better. He profoundly regretted coming to Corbin Hall.

This time, no one stopped them on the way out. In fact, they did not pass anyone at all. Better yet, the boy with the gig was still waiting outside, though both he and his horse gig had fallen asleep.

Peregrine eyed the narrow seat of the gig. "There won't be room for both of us." A one-horse gig was only intended to carry two people.

"I can sit behind," the boy said, "if you know how to drive."

Peregrine hadn't even noticed there was a seat for the groom behind the main seat of the little vehicle. "I will take the back seat," he offered, "because I do *not* know how to drive."

Roderick had once tried to teach Peregrine to handle a curricle and pair, but during the very first lesson, Peregrine overturned the curricle, giving Roderick a concussion, himself a sprained ankle, and the horses any number of scrapes and bruises. After that he had been content to leave the driving to someone else.

The ride back to the inn was rather horrible, since the groom's seat was not designed for comfort. Peregrine had not thought it possible for any horse to be slower than the hack he had borrowed a few days ago, but the nag pulling the gig seemed determined to prove him wrong about that. By the time they reached the Silver Griffin, he had a headache.

Even so, he fully intended to visit the nearest magistrate as soon as they had a chance to catch their breath and tidy up a little. He would very much have liked to change his clothes, but he could not, because they had not been able to retrieve his luggage.

Dora, to his surprise, refused to leave the inn. "We both need to rest, and we ought to eat something. I will write a note to the magistrate, asking him to call when he has the time. And in the meantime, you should lie down."

"I'm not tired," Peregrine argued. "And I haven't any appetite." Indeed, his pounding head made the thought of anything beyond a cup of tea nauseating.

She glared at him through narrowed eyes. "You were just kidnapped," she pointed out. "You had a terrible ride back to town under the hot sun. On top of that, you might be suffering from brain fever."

"I am not suffering from brain fever! Or any other fever! Is that even a real disease?" Before he could protest further, he saw that the corners of her mouth were curling up. Oh. She was joking, and he had taken her at her word.

"I suppose I can have a lie-down if you really think I ought to," he conceded. "But I don't really need to sleep."

"If you don't rest, I will start fussing over you," she threatened.

He shuddered. "Very well, if you insist." He wasn't sure what Dora meant by "fussing" but he felt certain that he did not want to learn. He did not particularly like being cossetted, even when he was genuinely indisposed.

Thus, Peregrine ended up lying in bed with a cold compress to drive away his lingering headache. He had doubts about the efficiency of so simple a remedy, but there was nothing else he could do while he waited for an errand boy to return from the apothecary. He did not take pain medication with him when he traveled. He knew his magical limits and seldom overextended himself when working spells. Unlike his friend Valance, he was rarely troubled by headaches for other reasons.

Given that he had spent several hours in a forced nap, Peregrine expected to lie fretfully in bed, worrying about what he ought to do next. Instead, for the second time that day, he fell into a sound sleep. He woke with his headache gone and his appetite returned a dozen times over.

It was just as well that he had recovered so fully, because the first thing he learned upon waking was that the magistrate had arrived and had many questions for him.

CHAPTER TWENTY-FIVE

ORA WAS EXCLUDED from Peregrine's interview with Mr. Lattimer, the magistrate. That was extremely annoying, since she could not help being curious, but she supposed it made some sense. She had not been there for Peregrine's confrontation with Mr. Blithfield, and she did not even know the name of the man she had ensorcelled. Her testimony would be of little use.

Mr. Lattimer did ask for her statement after he had taken Peregrine's, but he had few questions for her. She had far more questions for him—about the evidence against Mr. Blithfield, whether other guests at the house party were involved in their crime, and what the chances of conviction were—but he refused to answer most of them.

"All I can tell you is that the charges against the gentlemen at Corbin Hall will be taken very seriously." Then, much to her surprise, he smiled grimly. "Blithfield is my cousin, you know. On his mother's side."

"Oh dear. We have put you in a rather awkward position, investigating your cousin." Dora's heart sank. There might be no chance of a fair investigation if Mr. Lattimer was the magistrate in charge of the case.

"You need not worry about any conflict of interest," he said hastily. "I've suspected that he was up to something for quite some time. I just didn't know what. I quite hope that the charges stick. If he is in prison, he cannot keep bragging about his fly-fishing skills."

Dora took a moment to marvel at this level of pettiness before asking her next question. "Do you think he will go to prison?"

Mr. Lattimer's smile turned into a grimace. "He is more likely to receive nothing more than a fine. But we can hope!"

The magistrate reluctantly gave Dora and Peregrine permission to leave the county, though he warned them that they ought to stay within reach of the mail. "This is not the time to go jaunting off to Italy," Mr. Lattimer warned them. "Stay where we can find you."

"We will be in Surrey," Peregrine said, "at Carrington Abbey, near Haselmere."

Dora sent a sharp look his way; this was news to her. She waited until the magistrate left to ask about it. "Why did you tell we would be at the Abbey? I thought we were going to Keswick."

"Oh! After all that happened?" His eyes widened.

They sat in the inn's private dining room, at a table drawn up near a west-facing window. Afternoon light poured into the room. As she looked Peregrine full in the face, Dora noticed that the sunlight brought out the gold in Peregrine's eyes, rather than the green. It was a little distracting.

"I assumed we would both want to go home and rest," he explained.

"Oh." Dora frowned. "Isn't 'home' London?"

She and Peregrine intended to live at Carrington House, in Bloomsbury, not in the country. It was true that they hadn't had much time to plan their lives together, but she thought they agreed on that much, at least.

He looked down at his hands and shrugged awkwardly. "A person can have more than one home. Carrington House and the Abbey are both home. But," he added thoughtfully, "I suppose the Abbey is more home to me than the townhouse. It is where I grew up, after all. And my family is there. Everyone will be gathering for the summer holidays."

"Ah. I see." His relationship with his family was very different from her relationship with the Grantlys. Peregrine still had a mother; she did not. Which gave her an idea... "We can go to the Abbey, if you like, but I would like to take a brief stop in Kent first." Such a trip would be nowhere near as pleasant as honeymooning near Derwentwater, but it ought to be done, and now was as good a time as any.

"Kent?" Peregrine looked mystified, but only for a moment. Then his face cleared. "Ah, yes. Grantly Manor. Very well, we will visit your family first."

WHEN SHE LEFT Grantly Manor, Dora fully intended never to return. But coming back now, with her husband at her side, was quite different from being dragged back home by her guardians.

Who were no longer her guardians. Though Uncle Robert might still control her small fortune, they no longer had any authority over *her*. Dora fairly beamed with satisfaction when Peregrine handed to his card to the butler and added, "And this is my wife, whom you may remember as Dora Rossini."

Hulton's eyes nearly popped out of his head. "I most certainly do remember Miss Dora," he said. "My felicitations on your marriage, madame." By then, he'd gotten his expression under control. His real feelings about the elopement, whatever they might be, were concealed by his usual mask of polite professionalism.

Dora and Peregrine were left standing in the front hall while they waited to see if Lady Grantly was "at home" to them. Dora scanned the room with critical eyes. This was a handsome house, but it lacked either the comfort of Carrington Abbey or the elegance of Honora's townhouse.

Was it for this that Lady Grantly had been willing to sell her oldest daughter off to the Duke of Belmont? What a terrible bargain! No house was worth a human life. Dora's lips tightened as she remembered that Lady Grantly's dowry had come from her family's Jamaican plantation. If Lady Grantly was not shocked by the loss of human lives involved in the slave trade, perhaps it was not surprising that lesser evils did not faze her.

Before Dora could do more than begin to examine that thought, Hulton returned. "Her Ladyship will see you in the drawing room," he announced. "If you will come this way?"

Dora snorted. She did not need to be reminded of the location of the drawing room! She had lived here for eighteen years. But she forced a polite smile to her face and followed the butler. There was no reason to be rude to Hulton. She would save all her anger for her stepmother.

When they entered the drawing room, Lady Grantly rose to her feet, as elegant as ever. "Dora! What an unexpected surprise!"

The moment the door shut, she dropped her smile. Dora did so as well. Lady Grantly did not invite them to sit down. Evidently, the gloves were off.

"So, you have gotten yourself into another one of your scrapes, have you? I hope you do not expect us to help you out."

Another scrape? Dora gritted her teeth. "I have gotten married to Mr. Carrington. You can hardly call that a scrape."

"You married by eloping to Scotland." Scorn dripped from Lady Grantly's voice. "An elopement is a scandal in itself, as you ought to have known. Your sister was the talk of the county for weeks after she ran off with a stranger."

"I suppose I will be the talk of the county now," Dora said sweetly. "Everyone should be grateful to me for giving them something new to gossip about."

Lady Grantly's lips tightened. Before she could retort, Peregrine surprised Dora by speaking up. "Dora would not have had to elope if you and your brother-in-law had given consent for us to marry. May I ask why you were so opposed to the match?"

Dora raised her eyebrows. A very good question! How would Lady Grantly answer that?

Her stepmother hesitated for a moment; Dora suspected she was trying to come up with a plausible lie.

"I did not think it proper to reward your misbehavior, Dora," she finally said. "You put everyone's reputation at risk when you ran away from home. Does the family's good name mean nothing to you?"

"No," Dora snapped, "because I do not share the family name. You have never allowed me to use it."

Lady Grantly clenched her fists and glared. "If I had had my way, you would have been delivered to the foundling hospital," she hissed. "You should have been sent to live with others of your own kind, not raised alongside your legitimate siblings. But your father was entirely too sentimental, and—"

"Perhaps," Peregrine said softly, "Sir Isaac was not so much sentimental as he was fair. It was not Dora's fault that she was born out of wedlock. It was his. I am sure it was very awkward for you to have your husband's natural daughter living under your roof, but your anger seems to be misplaced."

Lady Grantly scoffed. Then she turned her face away. "Enough. I suppose you have won, Dora. We have nothing with which to negotiate now, and—"

"Negotiate for what?" Dora demanded. "Lord Valance has bought the mortgage to Grantly Manor. He was perfectly willing to forgive the debt. You were the one who refused to play along!"

"Merely forgiving the mortgage will not restore the family's finances." Lady Grantly sounded weary. "Everything your father left is held in trust for your brother and your sisters. I have no access to the capital."

Ah, so there it was. Valance was right to say that Lady Grantly was always after the main chance.

"Now," Lady Grantly said, "unless you have more to say, I must ask you to leave."

Dora drew a deep breath, set her shoulders back, and prepared to negotiate. "As a matter of fact, I do have one request."

"Yes?"

"I believe you still have my mother's jewelry, do you not? All of that belongs to me. I would like to collect that now."

Her stepmother sniffed audibly. "I suppose you will not give me any peace if I do not give you those damn trinkets. I warn you, most of them are worthless. But you may have them all. I would just as soon have no reminders of that woman in my house."

Dora sucked in her breath, but she made no protest against the bitterness in the older woman's voice. Peregrine was right about Lady Grantly's anger being misplaced. She ought to be angry at Sir Isaac rather than his mistress or natural daughter. Caterina Rossini had probably acted from necessity when she took a lover—so far as Dora knew, she had not been a particularly successful singer.

"I trust that is all?" Lady Grantly turned away from them.

Then Dora played her final card. "Actually," she said quietly, "you do have something to negotiate with. Honora misses Jack and the girls, you know." So did Dora, but she didn't want to reveal how much. "I believe that Lord Valance might be willing to assist his brother- and sisters-in-law if you allow for regular meetings between the families."

Lady Grantly stood rigidly still, but Dora could tell she was listening intently. "Lord Valance is a very generous man. I suspect he would be perfectly willing to cover the cost of the children's education." She had not forgotten that Belinda and Clarinda were to be kept home from school, or that Jack was going to be sent to an inferior school. "But he naturally would wish to know that his money was being used well." Dora doubted that Valance cared what school Jack went to, but Honora would care, and Valance would do nearly anything for Honora. "If you wish, I will speak to Lord Valance on your behalf."

That finally got a reaction. Lady Grantly looked back over her shoulder. "I believe something might be arranged," she said stiffly. "Though of course I will have to consult your uncle. Now, is that all?"

"Yes, I believe it is." Lady Grantly swept out of the room with a rustle of silk. Dora sagged with relief.

"That was clever of you," Peregrine whispered.

"Thank you." Dora tried for modesty, but failed. "I am rather proud of myself."

Some ten minutes later, Hulton returned with a footman in tow. The footman carried an impressive stack of wooden boxes. Dora sighed with relief. She had not quite believed that Lady Grantly would give her the jewelry.

"These are for you, Mrs. Carrington," Hulton said. "Shall I have them deposited in your traveling chaise?"

"Yes, please. And—Hulton?"

"Yes, miss?" He looked at her kindly. That was all the encouragement she needed.

"Are the other children doing well—Jack and Clarinda and Belinda? They are not being mistreated?" She watched him anxiously, praying he would tell the truth about something this important.

Hulton's face relaxed into faint smile. "They are doing as well as usual," he said dryly. "Sir Jacob is in trouble for filching jam tarts between meals, and Miss Clarinda is struggling with her mathematics lessons, but they are otherwise in fine shape. I will tell them you inquired, if I may?"

Dora breathed out a sigh of relief. "Yes, you may pass along my greetings to them. But please do not tell Her Ladyship that I asked about the children."

If he was surprised by that request, he hid his surprise well. "As you wish, ma'am."

When they settled back in the traveling chaise, Peregrine asked, "Why don't you want Lady Grantly to know you were inquiring about your siblings?"

Dora scrunched up her face. "Because I don't want her to realize how valuable they are as a bargaining chip," she explained. To Dora—and, she suspected, to Honora as well—Belinda, Clarinda, and Jack were worth more than all the diamonds in the

Crown treasury. But there was no need to tell Lady Grantly that. She would drive a harder bargain if she knew.

"I see." Peregrine looked almost sad.

This was all probably incomprehensible to him, Dora realized. His family would never treat each other the way Lady Grantly treated her children. A lump formed in her throat as she wished, not for the first time, that she'd grown up with a family as supportive as Peregrine's.

Dora did not want to become maudlin, so she switched to a more cheerful subject. "Your family is going to be so surprised to discover that you are married now!"

Peregrine stared blankly at her. "But didn't you tell them about the wedding when you wrote to Honora?"

"And spoil the fun? Certainly not! I wrote to Honora so she would know I wasn't dead, but I didn't mention that we got married." She chuckled. "I want to see the look on her face when she finds out I am a married woman."

Her husband continued to stare at her as if she had sprouted wings, the better with which to ascend to the heavens accompanied by a fanfare of trumpets. "Er, does your sister *like* surprises?" he asked doubtfully.

"I don't see why she wouldn't!" Dora argued. "Besides, it is only fair play. She ran off with Valance and got married without giving me the *least* bit of warning." Six months later, that still rankled. Honora should have trusted her enough to tell her about the plan to escape the Duke of Belmont! Dora was very good at keeping secrets.

"I suppose it would be hypocritical of her to scold you for eloping, too," Peregrine agreed. "Although the circumstances of their elopement were quite different. I'm not sure that Valance even liked Honora when he married her. He told me he did not think she was agreeable." He shook his head disapprovingly.

Dora narrowed her eyes, suddenly struck by a suspicion. "Did *you* think she was agreeable when you first met her?" It would not surprise her if Peregrine had fancied her older sister. Many gentlemen did.

"Of course! She is not nearly as interesting as you are, though. I mean, she is rather too conventional. And I don't like the way she wears her hair."

Dora's mouth twitched with amusement. "Would you like me less if I grew my hair out again?" She'd once had hair just as long as Honora's, though hers curled, whereas her sister's was straight.

"Why would you do that?" The very idea seemed to horrify him. "Of course, I would still like you if you grew it longer, but I think it is perfect the way it is now." Something about his expression shifted. "It was one of the first things I admired about you. But not the very first."

"What was the very first thing you admired about me?" Dora asked, fascinated by this glimpse into their first meeting. She expected him to say her eyes. In the past, other gentlemen had told her that she had beautiful eyes. Such a rare shade of blue, blah blah blah. By now it all seemed rather cliché.

But instead, he said, "I first admired your legs. And your bum. They look particularly good when you wear breeches, you know."

Dora burst into giggles, and it was sometime before she got her laughter under control. "You are adorable," she told him. "I hope you never change."

"No one can prevent changing. You never know," he said darkly, "I might start losing my hair, like Roderick. There's a patch as big as an egg on the top of his head, and it used to be only the size of a guinea." He shook his head. "He will be as bald as Uncle Matthew soon."

"I would still love you even if you become bald," Dora assured him. She had not meant his physical appearance, anyway. Rather than explain that, she leaned towards him and kissed him. After all, they had to do *something* to keep themselves entertained while on the road.

CHAPTER TWENTY-SIX

Mid-June, 1817

THE JOURNEY TO Carrington Abbey was slowed down by wind and rain, but by the time Dora and Peregrine rolled up in front of the Abbey, the rain had ceased. A single beam of sunlight broke through the cloud cover, illuminating the golden stone of the Abbey. A matching warmth flooded Peregrine's heart, and an automatic smile tugged at the corners of his mouth. He was home.

As it turned out, he was not the only Carrington who'd come back to the nest. Abigail and Susan had arrived a few days ago, bringing little Samuel with them. Abigail had high hopes that the fresh country air would do him good.

After Peregrine greeted his sister and her companion, he asked, "Has the baby been screaming as much as ever?" At the moment, Samuel was nowhere to be seen.

"No." Susan spoke in a hushed voice, as if she were revealing a solemn secret. "Your mother knows a colic recipe that actually *works*. And she is very good at soothing him. She can even get him to sleep in his cradle!"

"Some of the time," Abigail qualified. "Not during the day. But being able to put him down at night is a gift I'm quite willing to take." Her rueful grin shifted into a warmer expression. "He will be happy to see you again, Peregrine."

Peregrine scoffed. "I doubt he will remember me." Samuel was not even three months old yet. How good could his memory be?

Abigail lifted her chin. "He will recognize you," she insisted. "Simmons has already put him down for his nap, but you will get to see him when he wakes up. And then you will see that he remembers you."

If you say so, Peregrine thought. But he confined himself to a simple, "We will see." No need to antagonize Abigail by wagering money on it.

He barely had time to wash after his journey before a footman tapped at his door. "Begging your pardon, Mr. Peregrine, but Sir Roderick has asked to see you in his study as soon as you are able."

"I will be there shortly," Peregrine promised. He still took the time to change his clothes. It was early to dress for dinner, but he had a vague feeling that it would be best to look presentable in front of Roderick. More often not, a summons to the study meant something had gone wrong.

His hunch was confirmed when Roderick put aside the pen in his hand and gestured to a chair in front of his desk. This was not going to be a friendly conversation, then.

Roderick poured them both a glass of brandy. Peregrine accepted the drink, but set it down on the desk without tasting it. "Is something amiss?" he asked.

Roderick leaned back in his chair. "Amiss is perhaps too strong a word," he said judiciously. "I am, naturally, pleased to see you in good health. And it is good to see Dora again, too. But I must admit that I was rather surprised that you broke your promise about not eloping with Miss Rossini—though I suppose I mean Mrs. Carrington now."

"Mrs. Carrington-Rossini," Peregrine corrected. "I am changing my name too, you know."

Roderick raised his eyebrows, but said only, "The surname is immaterial to my point. I am sure I understand how, er, frustrating it must have been to wait on Robert Grantly's approval." He frowned. "I must say that Dora's guardians did not seem at all reasonable. I wrote to Mr. Grantly myself, laying out the case for allowing an early marriage, and all I got in response was a note saying he planned to charge us with harboring a runaway."

"Is that even a crime?" Peregrine protested. He had heard of people being jailed for harboring a fugitive, but not a runaway.

Besides, Dora was nineteen. Though she was a minor, she was not a *child*. Women married at younger ages all the time. His own mother had been only eighteen when she married his father, a much older man.

"I must say I don't know," Roderick admitted. "I doubt the Grantlys would ever have actually pressed charges, given that Lord Valance still holds the mortgage to their manor."

Roderick paused to sip his drink. "All of that is beside the point, though. What I meant to say was that I perfectly understand why you didn't like waiting to see if the Grantlys relented on the marriage issue. My objection is that you promised me you would not elope! I cannot ever remember your breaking a promise before, Perry. I did not expect that of you." He sounded. . . hurt.

Oh, dear. Why did these conversations always have to be so complicated? "I am sorry if I have offended you," Peregrine said. "But I didn't break my promise. At least, not technically."

Roderick swirled the brandy around in the glass. "Did you or did not promise you would not marry across the anvil?"

"I did not! I promised I wouldn't run away with Dora. And I didn't. She ran off to Carlisle on her own. I didn't elope with her." He had traveled with her across the border to Scotland, though. Did that count as eloping?

Peregrine frowned. Dora's explanation of why it would not be dishonorable to run across the border and marry had seemed convincing at the time, but now that he thought about it, there might be holes in her logic. Why hadn't he noticed them before? Probably, he guessed, because he wanted to keep sharing a bed with her.

"I really did think I was honoring my agreement with you,"

Peregrine told his brother. "Since we were already so close to the border, it simply made sense to get married." He could not really regret the decision, either. He *liked* being married to Dora!

Roderick covered his face with one hand. "I don't know how to explain to you how wrong that was. But at least promise me you will never do it again!"

"That would be an unnecessary promise," Peregrine pointed out, "since I am already legally married. Bigamy is against the law in this country. I am sure there are parts of the world that practice polygamy, but in England—"

Roderick broke into a rueful laugh. "I don't mean for you to promise that you won't get married in Scotland again. I certainly hope you will never have cause to do so! But I want to know that you will not break your word that way in the future."

"Oh, yes, I will try to avoid that," Peregrine agreed. "I hate breaking a promise. Though Dora possesses a certain flexibility of mind that allows her to follow the letter of the law without necessarily observing the spirit." He felt it only fair to warn his brother, since he could not predict what his wife might do next.

"Yes," Roderick said. "I can see that." He gulped down the last of his brandy as if he needed it. "It will be dinner time soon. Shall we go to the drawing room?"

"By all means." But the worried frown lingered on Peregrine's face. Was his mother going to scold him, too? Had he disappointed everyone in the family, or just Roderick?

He got his answer soon enough. Before he reached the drawing room, he met his mother.

"Peregrine!" She opened her arms up for a hug, and he bent his head down so she could kiss his cheek.

"I am glad to see you again, and doing so well," she told him. "And I am very happy to have Dora as part of the family now. She seems to suit you very well, my dear." The warmth of her smile made it clear she meant that.

Peregrine returned his mother's smile. "Yes," he said simply, "she does suit me." She was different from him in many ways, but their differences complemented each other, like citrus and cloves. He could not imagine any other woman who would suit him half so well.

By now, he had nearly forgotten about his sister's claim that Samuel would recognize him. But Abigail did not forget. When everyone had gathered in drawing room, Abigail brought the baby out to greet the new guests.

"Look who's here!" Abigail spoke to Samuel in a voice unlike the one she used for anyone else. It was as warm as the one she sometimes used for Susan, but more tender. "Your Uncle Perry!"

Samuel stared at Peregrine, his blue eyes wide with astonishment.

"See," Peregrine said, "he doesn't—" He was interrupted by a peel of infant laughter. Samuel waved his arms up and down.

"He remembers you!" Abigail crowed. She handed the baby to Peregrine.

"I suppose he does remember me," Peregrine marveled. Apparently, Samuel already possessed hidden depths.

When no one was looking, Peregrine brushed a kiss across the top of his nephew's fuzzy head. Samuel responded only by slobbering on Peregrine's clean dinner jacket.

Ah, well. No baby was perfect.

CHAPTER TWENTY-SEVEN

B Y THE TIME the butler, Morris, announced that dinner was ready, Dora had experienced what felt like a month's worth of emotions in a few hours. There had been the frustration over the bad weather that delayed their journey into Surrey; anxiety over how the Carrington family would react to the news of their marriage; and happiness at being reunited with these friends who had become Dora's own family.

As if all that were not enough, Lady Carrington had a surprise of her own for Dora. She revealed shortly after greeting her son and his new wife.

"Dora, will you come upstairs with me?" she asked. "There is something I would like to show you."

"Yes, of course, my lady."

"Oh, my dear, you need not stand on ceremony with me now that you are one of the family." Lady Carrington spoke cheerfully, but she cast an uncertain look over her shoulder as she led Dora up to the floor where most of the family bedchambers were located.

"What ought I to call you, then?" It was true that *Lady Carrington* sounded very formal, but many people did address their in-laws formally.

"I hope you will call me Mother, as Amelia does," the older woman replied. "But of course, you need not do so if you won't wish it. I will not be offended if you wish to continue calling me

Lady Carrington. Or you may call me Jane."

Dora shook her head. "I don't know. I shall have to think about it." She could not imagine calling a dowager baronetess *Jane*. And she had never called anyone *Mother*.

"Yes, do think about it," Lady Carrington said. "There is no need to decide now." She opened one of the bedroom doors and ushered Dora inside.

Dora glanced around. This was not the room she had stayed in during her previous visit to Carrington Abbey. Nor was it the room Peregrine had used. "Is this where Peregrine and I are to stay?"

"I have put you in the room next to Peregrine's, because I thought you might want your own space even though you are married." Lady Carrington lowered her voice. "If you ask me, I think married couples do better when they have space."

"I suppose so," Dora agreed.

So far, Dora had enjoyed sharing a room with her husband. In fact, she reveled in the pleasure of being alone with him. But it was true that Peregrine sometimes needed time to himself. The close confines of traveling together had worn on his nerves much more than on hers.

"I also wanted to show you this." Lady Carrington opened the wardrobe to reveal formal clothes: a black topcoat and a few crisp white shirts. They were too small to fit Peregrine.

"Oh, are those Cosmo's old things?" Dora guessed. Now that she'd studied the room, she suspected it used to be Cosmo's. The colors of the bedding and rug were similar to his room in London. No one else in the family seemed to care for those shades of brown.

"No, dear." Pink spots bloomed on Lady Carrington's cheeks. "I had these made for you, in case you ever wanted to wear something other than a gown at dinner. That is, I know you sometimes like to wear men's clothing, but I didn't know if you owned any gentlemen's evening wear, so—"

Dora interrupted her mother-in-law with a hug. "Thank you,

ma'am," she whispered. "I mean, thank you Mother." The word wasn't as hard to say as she'd expected. It would probably grow even easier with practice.

SAMUEL WAS TOO young to eat solid food, but at dinner time, the various members of the family took turns holding them while they ate. He seemed much less fussy than the last time Dora had seen him. Lady Carrington's baby-soothing magic must be powerful stuff. Dora made a mental note to ask her for the spell, in case Honora needed it in the future.

Abigail continued to crow about her victory over Peregrine. "We should have bet money on it," she said. "I *knew* Sam would recognize his own uncle."

"Or we could have wagered chores," Susan suggested. "When we get back to London, Peregrine can take on extra night shifts, as penalty for underestimating Sam. That would only be fair."

By this time, Dora was holding the baby, who was fascinated with her hair. Perhaps a little too fascinated: He grabbed a fistful of her curls and yanked painfully on them. Dora tried to pry his tiny fingers away, but it was surprisingly difficult. She didn't want to hurt him, so she couldn't be as forceful as she might have been with an older child.

"You know, when you go back to London, I could help you look after Samuel," Dora suggested. "I ought to do my part if I am to live at Carrington House."

Susan and Abigail exchanged glances. A cold lump formed in the pit of Dora's stomach. She and Peregrine had assumed they would live at Carrington House, but there had been no time to discuss that plan with his housemates. The house belonged as much to Abigail as it did to Peregrine. What if she objected to Dora moving in?

Dora darted a quick look across the table to see how Peregrine reacted. He looked supremely unconcerned. In fact, he continued calmly cutting his chicken into little bites.

Abigail, apparently, had no objections. She smiled at Dora. "That is an excellent idea. We shall have to clear out some of the books to make room, but we could use a sorcerer about the place, Dora. Three adults in the house are not enough to look after that child." She nodded at Samuel.

Samuel crowed with laughter again, as if the plan pleased him. Even better, he released the lock of Dora's hair so he could wave his hands enthusiastically. It was decided, then: Carrington House would have one more resident. And Dora finally had a family who claimed her as their own.

The End

Author's Note

Because the Cambion Club books incorporate fantasy elements, I allow myself more liberties in terms of historical accuracy than I usually would. The Cambion Club and the professional organizations for magicians (such as the Society of Astronomical Magicians) are all fictional.

There *was* a Foundling Hospital in London, founded in the eighteenth century by Thomas Coram. However, it did not operate the way the fictional Foundling Hospital in *Falling Star Enchantment* works. For example, there was no foundling wheel employed at the hospital for most of the institution's history, mothers had to deliver their children to the hospital themselves. Nor did the hospital place orphans for adoption. Those who managed the charity believed it was their responsibility to train the children for a life of work. Children who survived to their teens were usually apprenticed to a trade. Boys were sometimes sent into the military.

In real life, a foundling like Samuel would not have been adopted by a volunteer. Instead, he would have been sent to the country to be cared for by a wet nurse. Though the nurses often bonded with the infants in their care, many foundlings had short lives. In an era before antibiotics or an understanding of germ theory, infant mortality rates were high. Though mothers who surrendered their children often left notes or physical tokens by which the children could be identified, few children were ever reunited with their birth families.

You can learn more about the real-life Foundling Hospital at the website for Coram, the moder-day iteration of the charity founded by Thomas Coram in 1739. https://coramstory.org.uk/corams-history/the-foundling-hospital/

The Foundling Museum website also has information about the hospital, including a digital exhibit of some of the tokens left with the infants. https://foundlingmuseum.org.uk/our-story/history/

Acknowledgments

Because I began drafting The Cambion Club books back in 2022, I had help from many different people along the way. All three books went through significant revisions, and I am grateful for the assistance of numerous beta readers and sensitivity readers, including Petra P., K.C., Anne K., Sheila J., Juliette D., Sasha P., Amanda G., Cozy D., and Melissa S. I apologize if I have forgotten anyone!

Once again, I am particularly grateful to my autistic beta readers. When one reader suggested that Honora Grantly might be neurodivergent, I dismissed it; when a second one also suggested that Honora didn't seem neurotypical, I started asking serious questions about how I could have accidentally written an autistic-coded viewpoint character. Ultimately, this is one of the reasons I sought evaluation to see if I was autistic. (Spoiler: I am!) You might say that drafting this trilogy was life changing.

Although I won't name them, there were a few literary agents and editors who gave insightful feedback as to what they liked about and why they ultimately passed on the manuscript formerly known as *Runes and Ruin*. If any of you are reading this, know how much I appreciate the fact that you took time from your busy schedule to respond so thoroughly! I believe that *Twelfth Night Sorcery* is a stronger book because of these thoughtful rejections.

When I first began writing romance, I had no idea what to call my "Regency plus fantasy" books. I hadn't even heard the term "romantasy" yet, let alone "Gaslamp fantasy." The FaRo Society, the Fantasy of Manners FB group, and the "Lamplight and Steam" Instagram account have all helped me understand where my work fit into the broader genre of fantasy romance.

I am deeply grateful to all the staff at Dragonblade Publishing. These historical fantasy romances were very dear to my heart, and I am so glad they are finally out in the world! How awesome is it that Dragonblade now has an entire line dedicated to historical fantasy and paranormal?

Finally, I am grateful for all the readers who have purchased, borrowed, reviewed, or recommended the Cambion Club books. I hope you enjoyed them!

About the Author

Anne Rollins is the pen name of an English professor who lives in Northern California with her family, too many cats, and an enormous collection of books. She has spent untold hours of her life rereading Georgette Heyer novels, and hopes that someday people will compulsively reread her novels, too!

Join me at the following:
annerollins.com
facebook.com/profile.php?id=100094523334798
instagram.com/annerollins23
threads.net/@annerollins23

9 781969 349751